"Are We Going to Let One Small Mistake Ruin What We Have Together?"

"Michael," Alison pleaded as her heart raced. But her next words were cut off. His mouth covered hers too quickly for her to escape, and as they kissed, heat exploded within her, shattering the very fabric of the world itself. Her arms went around him without her willing them to, and even as his tongue met hers, everything—their arguing, their public fighting, and even his deception—faded from her thoughts.

"Now tell me you don't care about me," he said when he finally released her.

Dear Reader:

Romance readers have been enthusiastic about Silhouette Special Editions for years. And that's not by accident: Special Editions were the first of their kind and continue to feature realistic stories with heightened romantic tension.

The longer stories, sophisticated style, greater sensual detail and variety that made Special Editions popular are the same elements that will make you want to read book after book.

We hope that you enjoy this Special Edition today, and will enjoy many more.

The Editors at Silhouette Books

MONICA BARRIE
Lovegames

Silhouette Special Edition

Published by Silhouette Books New York

America's Publisher of Contemporary Romance

Lovegames is Dedicated To:
John and Denise,
With Love.

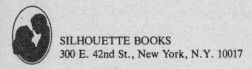

SILHOUETTE BOOKS
300 E. 42nd St., New York, N.Y. 10017

Copyright © 1985 by Monica Barrie

Distributed by Pocket Books

ISBN: 0-373-09243-1

First Silhouette Books printing June, 1985

10 9 8 7 6 5 4 3 2 1

America's Publisher of Contemporary Romance

Printed in the U.S.A.

MONICA BARRIE
a native of New York State, has traveled extensively around the world but has returned to settle in New York. A prolific romance writer, Monica's tightly woven emotional stories are drawn from an inherent understanding of relationships between men and women.

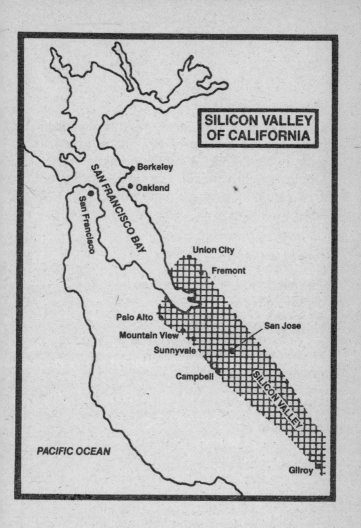

SILICON VALLEY
OF CALIFORNIA

Berkeley
Oakland

SAN FRANCISCO BAY

San Francisco

Union City
Fremont

Palo Alto
Mountain View
Sunnyvale

San Jose

Campbell

SILICON VALLEY

PACIFIC OCEAN

Gilroy

Chapter One

The television monitor showed the jovial, familiar face and penetrating eyes of the late-night talk show host. The sound was low, but Alison could make out the words clearly. Her nerves were on edge, and she forced herself to take several slow, calming breaths.

Why did I agree to do this? she asked herself for the hundredth time. But she already knew the answer—promotion.

She looked around the ultramodern room. They called it the "Green Room," although it wasn't green at all; it was done in soft shades of gray. The walls abounded with pictures of famous people: movie stars, authors, politicians.

There were two other people in the room, both of whom worked on the show. One was the assistant producer, a chic woman in her mid-thirties, wearing a severe dark-blue suit accented by a white scarf tied lightly around her neck. Her right hand was free; her left held a thick clipboard. The other occupant of the room was the makeup girl who had come in to check on Alison's makeup for any last minute changes.

Maybe it's not too late to back out.

"Miss Rand, Dan will be introducing you after the next commercial," said the assistant producer, motioning with her free hand for Alison to stand.

Too late, Alison told herself. Moistening her lips with her tongue and trying not to let the million nerve endings that were conspiring to paralyze her win out, Alison forced her body to follow her commands. She took one more deep breath and stood. Alison smoothed down the pale green skirt and adjusted the tailored waist-length jacket before following the other woman through the entrance to the sound stage. Just as she stepped from the Green Room into the outer edge of the studio itself, she heard the door open and close behind her.

Looking around, Alison saw a disordered maze of wires and cameras that defied description. In the center of the set were several comfortable-looking chairs on each side of the host's desk. The desk was pale wood set on an angle that would allow the host to see the guests with the least amount of leaning. An overhead monitor showed a commercial as the talk-show host, Dan Marshall, took a sip of water.

The assistant producer, lightly but firmly, grasped Alison's elbow and walked her to the edge of the stage. She smiled at Alison and winked. "Dan's a good interviewer. Try to relax and it will be over before you know it. When he introduces you, go to the desk, shake his hand and then sit on the seat next to him—to his right. You'll be on for eleven minutes before the first commercial."

Alison merely nodded her head. Even as she did, a technician came over and attached a small clip-on transmitting microphone to the lapel of her jacket.

As the technician worked, a flurry of activity erupted around her, and she knew that her first television appearance was about to begin.

Then Dan Marshall's melodic voice could be heard. "Tonight we have a special treat. Our next guest is Alison Rand, who, in the parlance of the high tech world, is a software writer. In fact, Miss Rand is the inventor, or author, if you will, of the number one computer game in the country, *The Wizard of Fantasy.* Alison Rand," he repeated and looked toward the curtain near the spot where she was standing.

"Have fun," whispered the assistant producer as she prodded Alison.

Squaring her shoulders and drawing herself to the fullest extent of her five-foot-two-inch height, Alison walked onto the stage and toward the host as the studio audience gave a smattering of applause.

From the moment she walked on the stage, shook Dan Marshall's hand, and sat down, her heart seemed to be pounding in her ears. She could feel the adrenaline racing in her blood. The first two minutes of her appearance passed in a nervous whirlwind of talk and smiles that Alison, no matter how hard she tried, would never be able to remember.

But when those first hesitant, nervous minutes ended, she was surprised to find that she was enjoying answering the questions the host asked.

As the assistant producer had promised, Dan Marshall was a good interviewer. He was able to get her to relax without appearing to be trying, and he had the ability to draw out her answers in a way that everyone could understand, rather than in the "computerese" she was used to speaking.

Time began to speed by, and Alison was able to ignore the cameras and the activity at the edge of her vision while she bantered with Dan Marshall and answered his probing questions.

From the corner of her eye she saw a woman wearing earphones hold up a prompt-card reading "one minute."

Even as she saw this, she heard an imperceptible change in the host's voice, and suddenly he asked the question she had been dreading. She had known it would be inevitable, and had rehearsed her answer a thousand times, but when he asked it, a wave of apprehension rippled within her.

"There is a growing concern," Dan began, "that computer games and video games are doing more harm than good to our children. That these games turn the children themselves into automatons."

"That's untrue!" she said in a much louder voice than she'd intended. She saw Dan's eyes widen in mock surprise, and caught the ghost of a smile at the corners of his mouth.

"In fact, just the opposite happens. You see, when someone begins to play these games—"

"Excuse me for interrupting, but rather than have you argue with me, I took the liberty of inviting someone who is qualified to debate this very subject, a man who feels that video games are destroying our educational system."

Alison fought to keep her jaw from dropping and show her shock. She realized she had been set up and there was nothing she could do about it. Instead, she gave a terse nod of her head.

"Wonderful," he said to her. Then he turned toward the studio audience. "Ladies and gentlemen, our next guest is a man who is well known for his activities on behalf of the American public. Let's welcome California's number one consumer advocate and the man *Time* magazine has called America's social conscience. Michael St. Clare!" The moment the host stopped talking, he turned toward the same curtains that Alison had passed through eleven minutes before.

Alison, like the rest of the audience, turned to look at the man striding purposefully across the stage. The instant her eyes met his, her breath caught. Something about the way he walked, the way he carried himself, assaulted her senses. His walk was graceful, and she intuitively knew that beneath the somber blue suit was a lean, well proportioned body.

His face was handsome, but even more so was the intensity she saw radiating from it. His hazel eyes gazed at her openly, and the strong angle of his chin told her even more of his character.

But overall, the man exuded an aura of masculinity that threatened to envelop her. Then he was shaking Dan Marshall's hand, and the host was introducing them.

Michael St. Clare offered Alison his hand, which she took. The moment their skin touched, Alison was aware of an instant burning that raced along her arm. She smiled hesitantly at him and then withdrew her hand before it was turned to ashes. But not once did she take her eyes from his. She had seen the slight flicker in his eyes when their hands had met, a flicker that had come and gone within the space of a single heartbeat.

When he finally turned and went to the chair on the other side of Dan Marshall, Alison began to breathe again.

"Michael, did you hear the question I posed to Alison?" Dan Marshall asked.

"A very apt one," Michael replied, turning his riveting gaze on Alison.

Alison stared at him, her heart beating faster than it should. His voice had the deep timbre of a trained speaker, and every syllable he'd uttered had vibrated through her body. Although she had never met him before, she had known of Michael St. Clare and his crusades on behalf of the American people. But she had never imagined him to be as physically powerful as he seemed.

"I've seen too many of today's youth subverted by senseless games," Michael stated.

"They're not all senseless!" Alison retorted. Anger at being set up to play a patsy had chased away the pulling reaction she'd had to Michael St. Clare himself. "Most of the new computer games are educational and help to train a young mind in the ability to concentrate."

"To concentrate on little round buttons that try to eat smaller little round buttons?" Michael asked.

Alison took a calming breath and shook her head emphatically. "For a child between four and fourteen, it teaches them eye-hand coordination and concentration."

"It doesn't help their vocabulary and social skills very much, does it?" Michael added.

"As a matter of fact," Alison said with a smile, "it does. It makes a child who has achieved a good score want to brag about it to his peers."

"And what about the violence it teaches? Besides

the cannibalism, what about the sheer joy of shooting down spaceships? Bombing cities? Destroying planets?"

Alison stared at him in disbelief. The tone of his voice, not the words themselves, added fuel to her slowly building anger.

When Alison spoke, her voice was cold. She stared directly into his eyes. "The games only follow the dictates of society, mirroring the world as it is. Listen to the news any night of the week; cities are bombed, people are murdered senselessly. Wars go on in small, underdeveloped countries. At least when a child plays a video game, only images are hurt, not people."

"But the violence of a game stays in the player's mind. It lessens the impact of real violence, makes it more acceptable," Michael stated.

"Does it?" Alison asked, but raced on before he could respond. "Is it more acceptable to see the special effects in a movie, when a man is shot and blood comes pouring out? Is it morally right that cartoons, specifically designed for children, are among the most violent forms of entertainment known? When you talk about mindless activity, just turn on your television any Saturday morning. At least with a computer game, the player has a chance to think, to react and possibly to change the situation. But in a show, there's no alternative. Movies and television are more mindless than any game I ever designed!"

"Excuse me a moment, folks, I hate to cut into this, but we have to take a station break." Dan Marshall looked straight into the camera. "We'll be back in a moment with round two of the 'Computer War'!"

Alison sat back and stared at both men. The host had a wide smile on his face, but Michael did not. In fact, Alison realized, he was studying her intensely with those deep, hazel eyes—so intensely that she started to feel uncomfortable.

"You're both doing wonderfully," Dan stated in an encouraging tone.

Alison broke Michael's stare and looked at Dan Marshall. "I think this whole thing is disgusting!" she whispered in a voice that only Marshall and Michael could hear.

"No," Dan Marshall said with a smile, "it's called show business."

"It's still—" but before she could finish, the signal came and Dan Marshall put on his television smile.

"Welcome back. For those of you at home who are just tuning in, my guests are Miss Alison Rand, a computer software designer, and consumer advocate Michael St. Clare. Tell me, Michael, why do you object to computers and their games?"

Michael favored the host with a half-smile. "I don't object to either. First of all, computers are playing an ever increasing and important role in society. Second of all, computer games do have their function. What I do object to is the tremendous emphasis given to these games, and the amount of time our youth spend playing them, rather than reading or studying."

"Miss Rand, how do you feel about that?"

Alison, although she agreed with some of the things St. Clare had just said, knew she could fall into a trap should she admit it. "With every change, there are detractors. The objects of bigotry are not confined to people. It seems that Mr. St. Clare is one of the bigots. I have never heard of a youth flunking out of school because he played computer games instead of football, a rather violent sport. And for your information, Mr. St. Clare," Alison said, her words dripping with sarcasm, "you must be able to read in order to play the games."

"Rudimentary reading skills are hardly what we're discussing. I cannot but think that these senseless games are destroying a student's ability to think creatively. After all, the games are programmed, and after the player learns the different maneuvers, then it's just routine."

Once again, Alison's anger tried to break free in the face of Michael's remark. "You're talking about the first and second generation simplistic games. The computer industry has changed greatly—is always changing. Games are no longer just simple manipulations of a joystick."

"Perhaps they should be. Then interest would wane, and life would get back to normal."

Her thin leash of self-restraint snapped at St. Clare's last salvo. His beautiful eyes no longer beckoned to her. The handsome, angular lines of his face dissolved under the fury of her temper. He had said the one thing that had pricked a tender, open wound. Gone were the television cameras, the audience and Dan Marshall as she retaliated.

"Normal? You mean they should fit into a mold. That everyone should stand in their own niche within the bounds of society's rules? Should everyone dress alike? Should we all read the same books? Go to the same shows? Own the same breed of dog? Perhaps we should stop thinking while we're at it." Alison stopped herself by forcefully taking a deep breath and sitting back.

Dan Marshall sat back too, a cat-that's-eaten-the-mouse expression on his face as he watched the two combatants go at it.

Michael St. Clare didn't even flinch at the anger

directed at him. He held her eyes in a steady gaze as he responded to her charges. "And what do you do? The same as most people who get involved with computers, I would bet! You go into your own private world, hiding from reality while you create diversions that can keep the real world and its problems away from you for as long as possible. You design your games and play them behind a wall of antisocial electronics! And you're teaching a whole new generation how to hide!"

Like an eagle spotting its prey, Alison reacted to his words with a swift attack. "You seem to have lost your objectivity, Mr. St. Clare. Why are you attacking me? You know nothing of my private life! Nor would I want you to! I think your arguments are biased and meaningless. There are more creative, advanced games that motivate the intellect than the mindless ones. But, seeing the position you've taken, I'm sure that you've never researched the subject thoroughly."

"Everything I do is thorough!" Michael stated, his temper flaring briefly before he controlled it.

Alison had seen the sparks flicker in his eyes, and noticed, too, a vein pulsing angrily in his neck. With the sense of survival that she had formed very early in life—a sense that had rescued her time and again—she knew that now was the moment to save herself.

"Spoken like a true egotist!" Turning to Dan Marshall, Alison spoke in a soft, sweet voice. "I'd like to stay and chat some more, but meaningless trivia always bored me, and I have a packed suitcase waiting for me to take it on a vacation." With that, Alison stood. She could not hold back the smile that sprang to her lips when Dan Marshall's jaw dropped. But strangely, she found herself disturbed by Michael St.

Clare's reaction. The angry flashes she'd seen in his eyes a moment before had turned to amused sparkles. And as she held his gaze her stomach suddenly felt like a cage full of butterflies.

Tearing her eyes from his, and without uttering another word, Alison walked off the stage and disappeared behind the curtains, conscious with every step she took that Michael St. Clare's eyes followed her.

Alison pulled the pillow over her head, but the constant and high-pitched ringing wouldn't go away. Irritably, she flung the pillow from her, sat up and stared at the telephone. As suddenly as her anger had come, it fled when she realized that the telephone was still disconnected. The ringing was her alarm clock.

She reached out one slim hand and pushed the button down. For two years she had promised herself she would get a new alarm clock, one that didn't sound like her phone. But each time she had been in a store, and looked at the clocks, she reminded herself that she had never been able to wake up to music.

Then she looked at her phone and wondered if she should reconnect it. Not yet, she decided. From the moment she had walked into her apartment the night before, the phone had not stopped ringing. Caller after caller had either congratulated her, or condemned her for what she was. The opinions, she had decided, had been evenly split.

I have to get an unlisted number now, she told herself. *Why did I ever go on TV?* But Alison knew the answer. Besides being paid a very nice salary, she earned a lot of money from royalties on her programs. Whenever she made a public appearance, it helped sell more games and generate more interest.

Until last night, she had only appeared at computer conventions, workshops and conferences. This had been her first true public appearance.

Shaking her head, Alison tried to rid herself of the fatigue that engulfed her. When she'd gotten home, long after midnight, she'd wanted nothing more than to go to sleep. Her anger at her own gullibility and at the talk-show host and Michael St. Clare had worn her out.

But the telephone had started to ring. Everyone she knew, and twice as many people whom she didn't know, had called. Some gave her praise, others backed up Michael St. Clare's views.

Michael St. Clare! He too was responsible for her tiredness; when she had shut off the phone at long last, undressed and slipped between the sheets, his face had loomed iridescently within the darkness. The handsome features, the air of power and masculinity, and the searching depths of his eyes had conspired to remind her of that first instant when their eyes had met across the stage.

It had taken her almost an hour to cast aside Michael St. Clare's image and to fall asleep. But with the new day's sunlight starting to filter into her bedroom, Alison realized that Michael St. Clare evoked unknown feelings within her mind and body and . . . Quickly, Alison stopped that train of thought.

Alison ran her hands through her short blond hair, and then left the bed. Three minutes later she stood under a spray of hot water, slowly waking up and joining the rest of the world.

When she was suitably alive, she stepped out of the shower, dried herself with a large terry towel, slicked back her hair and lavished herself with her one extravagance—a body powder she had discovered in a small boutique in Sausalito.

After emerging from the bathroom, feeling like a new and very pampered woman, Alison put on her underclothes and went to the closet to get the outfit she had chosen for the ride to the dude ranch.

For just a moment before dressing, she studied herself, and as it always happened, she had to blink twice before she actually saw her true image. What she did see with that first glance was a chubby, immature body that had been part of her curse for the first eighteen years of her life. By the second blink, she saw what she looked like now.

Without any more self-study, Alison reached into the closet and took down her clothes.

First she slipped on the pale blue polo shirt, her favorite type of casual top, and then pulled on a pair of loose white shorts. She never wore tight shorts, although she knew that she could. She liked the comfort of the looser shorts and the fact that they did not draw a lot of attention.

With a half-hour remaining until Sally would be picking her up, she straightened up the bedroom and went into the kitchen and put on a pot of coffee.

While waiting for the coffee to brew, she went into the living room. Standing in the center, she looked around. She loved her apartment with a passion. It had been the first one she had ever rented, and not once in the past four years had she regretted it. Originally she had taken the apartment because it was one of the few in the area that had a front entrance security system with an intercom.

The apartment was just large enough for her with its single bedroom, eat-in kitchen and overlarge living room, half of which was devoted to her at-home office. As a software writer, she had the option of working at home as often as she wanted, and was still able to use her company's vast resources via her computer and the telephone modem.

She had decorated the apartment in a way that blended the high tech of her computer equipment with the classic line of the traditional furniture she loved.

As she looked around the neatly ordered apartment, her eyes flicked to the two suitcases waiting near the door. When she'd walked off the t.v. show, she had not been lying. She was going on her first vacation in two and a half years, and she was looking forward to it.

A low bell rang and Alison went back into the kitchen. She turned off the gas under the percolator and when the coffee settled, she poured herself a cup. The lack of a coffeemaker was always joked about whenever she had friends over. No one could believe that a person in the computer industry refused to use the new computerized automatic coffeemakers. She always told them that she preferred her coffee perked.

Sitting down at the kitchen table, Alison took a sip of coffee and switched on the small portable television set. It was her only television, and she rarely watched it except for news and weather.

She turned on the weather channel and watched the national weather report. When they reached the resort areas in the California mountains, she listened intently. After the report, which called for a near perfect day, she shut the television off and finished her coffee.

Glancing at the clock, she saw that Sally would be arriving soon. Without any further delay, she rinsed out her cup and cleaned the percolator. Then she returned to the bedroom and checked to make sure the windows were locked, and all the lights were off. Just as she started out, she remembered the disconnected telephone and plugged it back in. Then she did the same thing to the phone in the living room. Not two seconds after she reconnected it, the phone rang.

Not again! she said to herself. She stared at the phone on her desk, debating whether or not to answer it. Shaking her head, she walked across the room and reached for the receiver.

As her fingers closed around the cool plastic, she heard the lobby intercom's low buzz. "Oh!" she cried, snatching up the phone quickly. "Hello?"

"Good morning," came a clear and distinctive voice that sent shockwave after shockwave racing along her spine. The deep timbre of the caller's voice was instantly recognizable, although she had only heard it once before.

"What do you want, Mr. St. Clare?" she asked as Sally rang the bell again.

"You."

"What?" She almost screamed the word as her mind fought to regain its suddenly lost equilibrium.

"I want to thank you for an interesting evening. I'd like to meet with you so we can continue our conversation of last night."

"Not a chance," Alison said, her voice tinged with an iron resolve she did not feel.

"Are you really going on vacation, or was that just your exit line? If it was, it was a good one."

"As a matter of fact, Mr. St. Clare—"

"Michael," he said quickly, cutting her off.

Alison's hand tightened on the receiver until her

knuckles turned a ghostly shade of white. A strange anger, mixed with an even stranger desire to see him, again overwhelmed her.

"Mr. St. Clare, I've waited two and a half years for this vacation, good-bye."

"Wait!" His voice held such authority that she surprised herself by actually waiting. "Alison?" he called in a softer voice. "Ms. Rand?" he tried again as Alison heard Sally knocking on her door.

"I have to go," Alison told him.

"Can we get together when you come back?"

Wavering dangerously as the memory of his handsome, well defined face rose up before her, she almost said yes. But then sanity returned; she thought of what he had said to her the previous night and the way he had so ruthlessly attacked her.

"I don't think so. After all, I do hide behind a wall of antisocial electronics." Alison smiled to herself after throwing his own words back at him.

"Give me one good reason why you won't see me," he said, his voice as calm as a summer breeze.

Alison wanted to hang up, but she knew that if she did, he would have scored a victory. "I'll give you two! Because you're the enemy and because you're a bug in my program. Good-bye, Mr. St. Clare, it was definitely not a pleasure."

With that, Alison hung up the phone and opened the front door to admit Sally Leigh, her one and only close friend.

"Ready to escape?" Sally asked.

"More than you'll ever know," Alison replied.

"But you're wrong, *Ms. Rand*, it was a pleasure," Michael St. Clare said aloud when he replaced the receiver on its cradle. If Alison Rand had acted differently during their short conversation, he would have been very surprised, perhaps even disappointed.

He didn't know why it had happened, but he knew that last night something within him had changed. It had changed the instant he had seen Alison Rand on the television monitor in the studio's Green Room, and it had happened again, in an even stronger way when he'd stepped onto the stage and greeted her.

Michael had used all his willpower to keep his face emotionless when he'd shaken her hand, knowing that at least a quarter of a million people were watching him. But the reaction he had felt toward Alison was something he'd been unable to deny to himself. In that moment which had seemed to stretch out for too long a time, Michael knew that Alison Rand was a very special person.

Closing his eyes, he thought about her. She was so totally opposite of what he looked for in a woman that he wondered what had come over him. She was much shorter than the women he dated—at least four inches shorter, which made her a good ten inches shorter than his own six-foot height. She had short hair, he loved long hair. Yet, she had the one inherent quality that he valued above all else. Strength.

From the moment he'd looked into her eyes, he knew he'd been caught by the mysteries he sensed lying behind their clear and crisp blueness.

Michael sighed as the phone on his desk rang. He ignored it, knowing that eventually someone in the outer office would pick it up. On the sixth ring, it was answered, but he was not aware of it; his mind was still lodged in the memory of the night before.

He had baited her, knowing that she was inexperienced in the art of television debate. He had wanted to see how thick her armor was, and had soon realized that he'd found several chinks. Yet she had retaliated bravely, and he'd soon found himself admiring her courage, even if he disliked what she was defending.

Then, as he always did, he drew on his reserves of strength and brought them into the battle, losing himself to the ideals he had come to defend, and tearing her arguments apart. He had sensed he was on the edge of victory, and was just about to leap forward with yet another barrage of accusations about the computer game industry when she'd turned the tables on him and walked off. She had not left the winner, but he knew he had not won either. The only true loser had been the host, Dan Marshall, who had sat for a full fifteen seconds with his mouth agape, staring at the spot where Alison had disappeared.

Michael had silently applauded her maneuver. And just as silently, he had promised himself that he would see her again. Michael knew that he had no choice. Alison Rand had affected him in a way no other woman had ever done before.

His intercom buzzed, but Michael ignored it. He was still picturing Alison's features. Her Cupid's bow mouth that was a perfect part of her face. The large, clear blue eyes, too inviting not to look into, were crowned by two symmetrical dark blond brows. Her small, pert nose with the smattering of freckles, that the makeup did not completely hide, gave reality to his vision. But her hair, he thought, should have reached her shoulders.

"And why," he murmured aloud, "couldn't you have been in another profession?" Sadly, Michael realized that of all the things that bothered him, the insanity that gripped the nation's teenagers was uppermost in his mind. He despised seeing anyone led about like cattle, especially the innocent children who would one day be running this country. And it was people like Alison Rand who were responsible for those things happening.

Michael knew he was one of those rare people who believed in himself and in what he did. He had discovered that within him there lived two vastly different people. The Michael St. Clare who loved life and enjoyed everything about it, and the Michael St. Clare who watched everything around him and saw so much that was wrong.

It had started in college, where he had been a sociology major. By the time he'd graduated, he had learned that he would never be satisfied with the state of most of the world. He saw too many things that were wrong, too many unfair practices and too many people being hurt for no reason except profit.

People everywhere suffered from the greed and avarice of big business. Under the twin influences of his new revelation, and of a personal tragic reality, he had become a modern Don Quixote, fighting against the windmills of big business.

He'd joined the small ranks populated by Ralph Nader and others of the same ilk, and found that, although it was satisfying to go up against big business, it was always a hard-fought and rarely-won battle.

With each victory against those who would cheat, or even harm their customers, he felt that he had indeed chosen his path wisely.

Michael was more than just a consumer advocate, he was a sociologist, and recognized certain patterns in society's behavior. Besides going after big business, Michael had always made it a point to try to protect the public from changes that had always been considered safe or good. The educational system, and its degeneration, were prime targets for him. The medical world was another community to which the public seemed to give implicit trust, and a community that Michael watched closely for those who did not or could not.

When he had reached his twenty-eighth birthday, he had seen a new trend developing, a trend that was a danger to everyone. With very little notice, big business had shifted its primary target from the adults who spent their hard-earned salaries, to the teenagers, and even preteens, who were the next generation of wage earners.

Michael had recognized the signs early and had tried to convince everyone he could about their portents, but few rallied to his banner.

Over the past three years, he had started to gain favorable support, especially in light of the epidemic-like spread of t.v. video games and of the video game parlors that had cropped up everywhere across the country.

For the nine years he had been a consumer advocate, Michael had devoted himself to his work, taking only a minimal amount of time for his own life. Although he dated, he did so infrequently, and only when he was not in the midst of a battle. When he was working, he had little time to spare to think of other things. Invariably, whenever he had formed a relationship, it had fallen apart because of a lack of understanding that his work was a large part of his life, not just a job that could be turned off when he left the office.

Michael swiveled his chair and looked out at the San Francisco skyline. He tried to clear his mind of all thoughts—of consumer advocacy, last night, and Alison Rand—but he found the task impossible. *Some-*

how, he told himself, *somehow, I will make her understand what she's doing.*

"She has to," he said to the haze-shrouded outline of the Golden Gate Bridge. Suddenly, Michael turned the chair again and pressed the talk-bar on the intercom. "Anne, get me everything you can dig up on Alison Rand. Everything!"

When he released the intercom, he smiled. Anne was more than just his assistant, she was his top researcher. She had been with him since the beginning.

Michael was certain of two things: within twenty-four hours, at the most, he would know more about Alison Rand than even her mother did; and, he would not let her out of his life.

Chapter Two

Alison, feeling refreshed after her shower, wrapped the large terry towel around her and stepped into the well-appointed hotel room. She paused after her second step to look for Sally.

"I'm off," Sally said from the doorway.

Turning quickly, she found Sally standing in the partially open doorway. "Off to where?"

"Scouting."

"What?" Alison asked, her face emphasizing her puzzlement.

"What else? It's time to look over the men we'll be sharing our vacation with."

"We just got here," Alison protested.

"And therefore we shouldn't waste any more time. Alison, I've already told you that I have no intentions of spending my entire vacation sitting next to you," Sally reminded her with a smile that negated the

harshness of her words. "Besides, you promised me!
So, get dressed and meet me at the Spur."

"The Spur?"

"The lounge. I want to check out the eligible
candidates. Don't take too long."

"I won't," Alison responded without much enthusiasm, but her tone did nothing to dampen Sally's
dazzling smile.

When the door closed, Alison shook her head. It
wasn't that Sally was a man chaser. In fact, it was just
the opposite; Sally Leigh was one of those extraordi-
nary women who attracted men without trying. She
had the tall, lithe body of a ballerina, and the classic
beauty that went along with it. No, Sally was only
doing what she always did—trying to get Alison to
come out of her shell and join the world.

Alison and Sally had been friends for a long time.
They'd met when Alison had first come to the budding
area known as Silicon Valley. She had just turned
twenty-one and had graduated from college.

Their friendship was one of those rare things that
happen between two people who have nothing in
common. Yet, from the moment they had first talked
together, they had found themselves enjoying each
other's company.

From that point on, they had gotten together fre-
quently. And Sally had appointed herself Alison's
official matchmaker, no matter how hard Alison protested.

For a full year she had argued and fought with Sally,
but to no avail; Sally was every bit as stubborn as
Alison. Eventually, Alison's persistence won out, and
Sally had stopped trying to make a match and accepted Alison at her word—that Alison didn't want to
be involved with any men at that time.

But now, three years later, Sally was starting all over again. When Sally had invited Alison to join her on this vacation, Alison had agreed, knowing that she was in desperate need of a rest. After she had told Sally so, she'd seen a flashing smile of victory.

"But only if you'll enjoy yourself with the other guests. A dude ranch is for mixing," Sally had declared.

"We'll see," Alison had responded vaguely.

"No, ma'am!" Sally had snapped. "I don't intend to spend two weeks staring at you while you hide."

"You won't have to stare at me!" Alison retorted, but Sally had gone on unperturbed.

"But I will, you know that. Besides, there'll be plenty of men there. Please, Alison, don't back away this time."

Alison, not wanting to fight with Sally, had agreed to the deal. And nothing else had been said until just now. Shrugging away her helplessness, Alison went over to one of the twin beds and lay across it.

She was feeling much better than she had when they'd started out from Silicon Valley early in the morning.

They had made the drive to the mountains a leisurely one, and it had worked the magic that Alison had hoped it would—only, of course, after Alison had spent the first half-hour carrying on about Michael St. Clare's unwarranted attack on her and her profession. She repeatedly described to Sally, in the minutest of detail, how she had been set up by the television show and probably Michael St. Clare as well.

But with each mile that had fallen behind them, she'd shed her anxieties. The beauty of the California countryside worked its soothing balm on her troubled mind, and she'd soon forgotten the long days of nonstop work which had marked the last four months of her life.

She had also pushed aside the memory of Michael St. Clare along the way. But, even as she gave birth to this thought, his handsome face, capped by a thick, almost unruly mass of curls came instantly to mind. Her body, so relaxed until then, tensed.

Stop! she ordered herself. Sitting up, Alison took a deep breath. She stood and walked to the dresser, where she had already laid out a matching bra and panty set, and put them on.

Looking at her reflection in the large mirror she suddenly froze, and tried to shake away the sensation that she was staring at someone else. But the woman in the mirror had her eyes.

At twenty-four, Alison knew she should be used to seeing herself. But it was always a shock to realize that the woman in the mirror was herself; she was no longer the person who never fit in anywhere.

But I do now, she told herself as her eyes traced the outline of her body. Although she was not tall, her legs and torso were perfectly proportioned. Her sleek calves blended into firm, perfectly rounded thighs. Her hips flared in a gentle arc which accented her slim waist and proudly upthrust, if not large, breasts.

So different, she told herself. *I'm so different.* Then she thought of Michael St. Clare's remark about life being normal, and her angered reaction. Without wanting to, Alison's mind called up the memories she had so forcefully shut away from her consciousness— memories of her unhappy childhood, of the chubby girl who did not fit in with the rest of the kids.

High school had been the worst. She'd had two

things going against her; she was short and pudgy, and she had brains—that and the fact that going to school with a large student population did not lend itself to making friends if you did not fit into the accepted mold.

While all the other girls seemed to change daily before her eyes, growing taller, sprouting breasts and flaring hips, her body never seemed to change. It had gotten to the point where Alison had refused to look at herself when she dressed, unable to stand the sight that had always awaited her.

Alison had tried diet after diet, exercise plans that guaranteed her a perfect figure, but nothing worked. No diet was ever able to change her frumpy-looking body. She had gone to the doctor, after begging her mother to take her, and the doctor had run all manner of tests. His results had defeated her as much as anything.

"You have a slow metabolism. That's all it is."

"Can't I take something for it?" she'd asked.

"No. But it may change one day." The doctor had held up the frail hope for her, but Alison, disappointed so often, had refused to accept it.

She had no friends, for who would want to be associated with a girl who looked like a too-short center for a football team? The boys had ignored her completely. They didn't even tease her or pick on her. At times, Alison had prayed that they would do something, anything, except ignore her.

Her mother had tried to comfort her, but without success. How many times, Alison had wondered as a fourteen-year-old, could someone tell her that she would grow out of it soon?

Alison had turned inward by the tenth grade,

seeking ways to hide from the world, and to be protected from her lonely existence. Part of her escape had been found in her studies; her devotion to them pushed her grades to the top of the class.

But there were only so many hours in the day for her to study. She still had to face the world at other times, and craved some sort of companionship. One afternoon, as she had wandered along the science laboratory corridor, she passed the partially opened door of the computer lab. Pausing, she glanced in.

The room was a jumble of equipment and blinking red lights that had called to her in an ethereal, compelling way. She was attracted, too, by the activity that had seemed to charge the very air itself.

There were five boys, each one sitting before a computer console, their fingers flying over the keyboards like a typist gone mad. Fascinated, Alison had slowly entered the lab. She had picked a spot behind one boy and watched as his fingers gave the computer its commands and the monitor's screen came alive.

She had studied everything he did and watched as a problem he had entered into the computer came up and then resolved itself.

Without her realizing it, the boy she had been standing behind had turned to look at her. "Interested in computers?" he had asked.

"I don't know," Alison had replied honestly.

"Most girls aren't."

Alison had thought about that statement for several seconds. "I guess I'm not like most girls, then," she had stated. "Would you . . . would you show me a little about it?"

That had been Alison's first experience with computers. It had also been the first lesson she had learned about computer people. People who were involved with computers seemed more readily able to accept another person, no matter what the person looked like, as long as the interest was genuine.

And Alison's interest was not only genuine, it became all-consuming. Each day after classes she would go into the computer lab and sit with the boys—she was the only girl in school who did. She learned everything they could teach her with the greed of someone too long denied.

Within six months, Alison had become the equal of any of them in programming. She had found her world, a world in which she could disappear whenever she wanted. The escape into another dimension had been the one thing that had saved her from the self-pity at her inability to change her looks.

At the end of eleventh grade, Alison was the resident computer genius of her school. She had also written several programs that had been sold for enough money to buy her own computer.

By the time Alison had graduated from high school, her body still as chunky as ever, she had earned sufficient money to pay for college. But she had not needed to use that money because her talent had been recognized. She had been awarded a full scholarship to study computer sciences at Stanford University.

When Alison had arrived at Stanford, she had found herself sharing a room with one other girl. As had been her habit, she remained hidden in her own private shell. She had developed this protection to insure that she would not feel left out. Although it helped her to survive, it did absolutely nothing to cultivate friendship.

After a few weeks, Alison learned that college was

vastly different from high school. The students were there to learn, study and prepare for their futures. Slowly, Alison had begun to lower some of the barriers that kept the others away from her. When she did, she realized that she was being accepted for herself, and not for what she looked like.

Yet, during her freshman year, while all the other girls in the dorm dated, especially her roommate Lauren Frisch, she was never asked out. But by the middle of the second semester, she and Lauren had a nice, comfortable relationship.

One time Lauren had fixed Alison up with a blind date, against Alison's strongest protests. She had refused to tell Lauren that she had never dated, and finally had to give in under the pressure Lauren exerted. The evening had been miserable, and she had realized that her date was only doing Lauren a favor. He had been very nice to her, taking her to a movie and dinner, but she had sensed that it was a chore for him, even though he pretended to be enjoying himself. After that, she had not dated again.

When her freshman year was almost over, Alison had realized that she loved California, especially after growing up in Fort Lee, New Jersey, a stone's throw from Manhattan. For the first time in her life, she felt restless and in need of doing something more than studying.

During that spring she had decided to look for a summer job, a job that did not involve computers. One Sunday morning, three weeks before the end of the school year, she had been scouring the *San Francisco Chronicle,* looking for odd-type jobs that might pique her interest, when Lauren walked into the room.

She asked what Alison was thinking about doing, and learned that she wanted to get a summer job in California.

"My father always hires several students during the summer. I could ask him," she had volunteered.

"What would I do?"

"What I do every summer, work on the ranch."

"But I don't know anything about working on a ranch," Alison had protested.

"You can learn. Think about it, but please don't take too long. I'll tell my father to hold a spot for you for a few days."

Alison had thought about it. It was so completely different from anything she had ever imagined doing that the idea began to intrigue her. Twenty-four hours later she told her roommate that she would take the job if Lauren's father was willing.

When school ended, she went home for a week, and then returned to California—Southern California—and started to work on her roommate's father's ranch.

Although the work had been hard, Alison had thrown herself into it greedily, learning that the warm sun and the beautiful countryside were pleasures she had never known before. Within a few weeks she had become proficient with many of the chores, and had learned to ride fairly well.

By the end of the first six weeks of the summer, something else began to happen to her. At first she hadn't realized it, but then she found that her clothing was beginning to hang on her like bags.

Startled by this sudden change, Alison began to look more closely at herself. Then she discovered that her body was changing. The chunky body she had always striven to ignore was starting to redesign itself.

By the end of the summer, without the aid of a diet, Alison had gone from a size thirteen, to a size nine. When she returned to college for her sophomore year, she did so with an entirely new wardrobe.

Yet, no matter how much she had tried to tell herself she was changing, eighteen years of seeing a fat person in the mirror was a hard habit to break. By the end of the first semester, still without trying to diet, her body had continued to change. The change was so evident that Alison had grown nervous and visited one of the school doctors.

After the doctor had run a battery of tests, he had told Alison that there wasn't a thing wrong with her.

"Then why am I losing so much weight?"

"The only reason I can think of, is that you've been undergoing a metabolic change. You did say that your metabolism had always been clinically low?"

"Yes."

"Then be happy, because it's normal now. Enjoy it!"

Normal! The word had echoed in Alison's ears endlessly. She was normal now. Her figure no longer resembled that of a football center, and her clothing actually showed the curves of her body, in the places they were supposed to be. She should have been happy, but she wasn't. Alison had spent too many years avoiding herself, and when she'd lost all her weight, she'd still been unable to see the new person whom she had become.

Once again, Alison had retreated into her shell, and had thrown herself deeply into her work. The only differences in her life had come with the onslaught of phone calls asking her for dates, which she had turned down, one after another, without qualm.

Lauren had tried to shake her free from the hold that the past had on her, but even she was ineffective and had soon stopped trying.

The next two years had passed in an obsessive ritual of study, and of working on new programs that would enable her to make her entrance into the world of computers.

Then in her senior year, things had changed again.

The loud ringing of the hotel room's phone broke Alison out of her trance. Shaking her head, she realized that she had been lost in the past while she had stood staring into the mirror.

Moving quickly, she grasped the phone. "Hello?"

"Are you being fitted for a formal gown?" Sally asked. "I've been waiting for a half-hour."

"Five minutes," Alison promised before she hung up the phone and locked her memories into that special place where she always kept them.

"You're sure?" Michael asked as he leaned back in his chair and stared at Anne Harding, his assistant, who had just put a manila file folder on his desk.

"Absolutely," she replied.

"You called the stations and gave them the hints?"

"John Lawson is the host of the 'Afternoon Show' show. He's also a friend of mine. I told him what we wanted to do, and he thought it would be a great idea. Especially after Dan Marshall's show drew so much interest."

"Now all we have to do is get Alison Rand to agree."

"Why her, Michael? Why not find someone else?"

"I don't want anyone else," he stated. He saw Anne's puzzled look, but refused to be drawn into an explanation.

"We'll have to get her to agree to do the shows as soon as possible. John wants to set his schedule, which he says is very tight, and he wants you to know he's doing this as much for the show as he is for me."

"That's very noble of him, especially if his ratings go up. Did you find out where she went on her vacation?"

"Not yet. It'll have to wait until morning. It's almost seven, and Tri-Tech Corporation's offices are closed for the night." Anne paused for a moment and then shrugged her shoulders. "I'll see you in the morning."

"Night, Anne," Michael said absently as she left the office and he reached for the file. A moment later he was immersed in the information Anne and his staff had found about Alison Rand.

It was an hour later when he looked up and realized that the light was gone from the sky. Shrugging, he leaned back, contemplating her circumstances.

Alison was twenty-four years old and had three degrees. The first was her bachelor of science from Stanford. The second and third were master's degrees in related fields of computer science.

Alison Rand, Michael realized, was a very smart lady—as far as books were concerned. Her file contained a lot of information, but little of it was of any real help. She had started working for Tri-Tech right out of school, and if his figures could be believed, her salary made a bank president's look like chicken feed.

Yes, Alison Rand is a very valuable asset to Tri-Tech, he thought. But he knew it was more than just her intelligence that made her so valuable. The information had also revealed that Alison had won several top awards in her field, and along with writing game programs, she had also written many medical programs, one of which enabled neurosurgeons to be more accurate in diagnosing and treating certain forms of tumors.

Still, her most important contributions to Tri-Tech Corporation came in the form of her computer games, which had put Tri-Tech on the verge of becoming a leader in the home television game market.

But, Michael pondered, there was nothing at all about Alison Rand the woman. The only information Anne had been able to gather had been on Alison Rand, the computer genius.

Why? Then Michael smiled. He had been aware of Anne's curiosity about why he wanted to debate Alison Rand, and no one else. For the first time since he had chosen his path as a consumer advocate, he was using it to do more than make the public aware of what was happening around them. He was using his position, and his power, for himself too.

"Why does she have to have short hair?" he asked aloud.

Alison stood off to one side, gazing at nature's most beautiful palette, the sunset. From the distance, the other guests of the Tall Pass Dude Ranch were enjoying the buffet to the fullest. But Alison wasn't interested in the others, she was happy to be where she was, leaning against the fence and relaxing for a change.

After quickly dressing and joining Sally at the bar, she'd sat and listened to her friend's appraisals of the men around them. Sally had already determined, she told Alison, the three men whom she would allow to become friendly with her.

"And the three men I've chosen for you—"

"Sally—"

"Are very interesting, and handsome to boot," she'd finished as if she hadn't been cut off.

Without really protesting against the inevitable, Alison had followed Sally's lead. A few minutes later the first of the men, who had somehow picked up Sally's signals, wandered over to them.

An hour later they had found themselves eating dinner from the western buffet and sitting at a small table for four. Alison's date was a banker from San Diego; Sally's was a television executive.

Alison had to admit that she had started to enjoy herself. The conversation was light, centering around the activities available at the ranch, in which the men had been participating for the last four days.

When the topic had focused on work, and the man sitting next to Alison had asked what she did, she'd seen his eyes waver for just a moment when she told him.

"I didn't know women went in for that sort of thing," the man had said to her. Alison had smiled to herself. As a rule, most men seemed to think that computers and women were incompatible.

Alison had cast an amused glance at Sally, who had been listening intently to the conversation. She saw too the warning glint in Sally's eyes, but refused to yield to it. *If she wants me to date, then she has to take the good with the bad,* she told herself.

"Why not?" she'd asked.

"Well . . . you know."

"No, I don't," she'd replied, keeping her voice soft and amiable.

"Well, women never really show an aptitude for math and computers."

"There's always an exception to the rule," Alison replied, holding back the spark of anger at his biased words. "Besides, psychologists have discovered that it isn't women who don't have the ability for math, it's the people teaching them who think that way."

She had seen that her date was not slow on the uptake, and had wisely changed the subject.

"Does your profession pay well?" he asked. Even as he spoke, Alison heard Sally choke on the drink she had been sipping.

After Sally had recovered, Alison shrugged her shoulders. She already knew he had classified her as a woman in a man's field and, with that, had negated any possible high income. Before she answered, she had glanced again at Sally and had seen the warning shake of her head. In spite of the fact that she knew better, she couldn't help smiling.

"It pays well enough for those who know what their doing. But I was a little disappointed last year, I had expected to earn a little more."

"That's terrible!" the banker commiserated, but Alison did not sense any real emotion from the man. In fact, his tone, and the falseness of his words, seemed more smug than sorry. His whole attitude was an "I thought so" type of oversecure attitude. Irritated by his flippant manner, Alison loosened the restraints she'd placed on herself.

"It's not terrible," Alison had told him with a straight face. "I put ten thousand dollars into my retirement fund, invested another twenty thousand in the market, and whatever I didn't spend to live on, I put into my savings. . . . I don't do too many frivolous things."

As she spoke the man's face blanched, and she'd

known she had broken the silent rule that a woman could not earn more than the man she was with.

"I . . . I didn't realize that—"

Feeling genuinely sorry for the man, and regretting that she had pulled this on him even though she thought his smugness had warranted it, Alison cut off his apology. "Why don't you tell me more about the ranch?" she asked.

But as the man spoke, the high spirits that had been a part of the table's conversation had disappeared, and by the time they'd finished eating, he had excused himself. Alison had left too so that Sally could enjoy her time with her date.

"Why did you do that?" Sally asked, startling Alison, and taking her mind from the multicolored horizon.

"I really am sorry," she told Sally. "As soon as it happened, I felt bad."

"Damn it, Alison, why do you always do something like that? Why do you chase them away?"

"I don't know," she said in a low voice.

"Don't lie to me."

Alison stared at Sally for a long time. Her friend had never before said something like that, or used quite that tone of voice. Taken aback, Alison began to draw on her old defenses.

As soon as Sally saw Alison's eyes waver, and saw too the way her shoulders began to slump, she knew she had struck a deeply imbedded nerve. "Alison, I'm . . ."

But Alison stopped her from going on. "It's all right, Sally," she said, her voice cooler than she'd meant it to be.

Sally shook her head stubbornly. "No, it's not.

Alison, we've been very good friends for a long time. I don't want anything to change that. But damn it!" she snapped, suddenly feeling the emotions that were an integral part of her friendship for Alison, "I love you and I want to help you."

"Help me?" Alison echoed, turning away from Sally and back to the last vestiges of the sun.

"Alison, in the last three years, I've learned a great deal about you. I know what your life was like when you were growing up. You shared that with me. You told me about the pain and the hurt, and about feeling different from everyone else. But that's in the past. You're a beautiful woman now. A woman who can have any man she wants. What are you so frightened of?"

Sally's last question was asked in a low voice, almost a whisper. But to Alison, it was as loud as a shout. Unable to prevent it, tears spilled from Alison's eyes and trailed along her cheeks. One reached the corner of her mouth, and as she tasted its saltiness she turned back to Sally.

"I didn't realize I was frightened of anything until you said so," she told Sally.

"Alison . . ."

"It's all right, really. And you're right also. I am afraid of men."

Sally saw the tortured depths of her blue eyes, and grasped Alison's hand. "I didn't mean to bring up painful memories."

Alison's dry laugh sounded false. "Yes, you did. You want to help me. You want to know why I do the things I do."

"No," Sally said, "I don't care why you do them. I just wish you'd give yourself a chance to be happy."

"But I am," Alison protested. "I have everything I want. A job that I love, work that I can lose myself in and an apartment that is all my own."

"And what about love?"

Alison took a deep breath and shook her head. "For what? To disrupt my life? To make me become subservient to a man? To hurt me? No, thank you, I like my life just as it is."

"You mean you like the safety you've found in your life."

"You're so different, Sally. You don't let a man take over. You don't let a man hurt you. When a relationship is over, you just go on your own way. You don't get hurt."

"Don't I though," Sally whispered. "Alison, when you let your emotions free, sometimes you do get hurt. I've been hurt badly, but I keep trying. I don't let it show, because I know that one day I'll meet a man I can love, and who loves me without reservation. But the only way I'll find him is to keep looking."

Alison listened to Sally's impassioned words, and realized that she had been wrong about her friend who always seemed so carefree. "You're so sure," she said.

"I have to be! I won't give up that hope of being happy and of sharing my life with someone I love."

"I wish I could think like that."

"You can try, but first you have to get rid of whatever ghost is haunting you."

"I've tried," Alison admitted.

"No, you haven't. You've hidden yourself away is what you've done."

Alison shook her head against the truth of Sally's

words, but they kept striking at her, over and over again, long after Sally grew silent.

Suddenly Alison squeezed Sally's hand and looked into her eyes. "All right, I'll try. But, how do I start?"

"By talking about it. By bringing it out and letting it free to leave you."

"My friend the psych major," Alison tried to joke.

"Only one year, remember. Talk to me, Alison. Try."

Alison looked at the spot where the sun had fallen and wished she could follow it. But at the same time, she realized that Sally was indeed her friend and was trying to help her. Slowly, Alison nodded her head.

"It feels like it was ages ago. I was a senior at the time," she began, doing her best to control her voice and keep as much emotion out of it as possible. Yet even as she spoke, the pain of that time returned to wrench at her heart. "His name was Stephen Palmer. He was one of my professors. If it didn't hurt so much, I would think it was funny. There are always so many stories about teachers and students. . . . I guess I'm one of them now. I met him on the first day of class in my senior year. I . . ." Alison paused to take a steadying breath before she continued.

"I had never been attracted to anyone before, but something about him attracted me. He was handsome, but he was also so much more mature than any of the students I knew. After a few weeks, we began to talk to each other after class, or when we'd bump into one another on campus.

"Then one day, we were both walking toward the administration building. He asked me out for dinner, and for the first time I heard myself answering with a yes.

"It was a night I thought I'd always remember. We had a wonderful dinner, and then all we did was walk around the campus until midnight had come and passed, and he escorted me to my dorm.

"We started seeing each other a lot. When the semester ended, and my course with him was finished, I thought I was in love. What I was, was stupid and naive."

Alison stopped then to look at Sally, who had stayed silent throughout her monologue. She waited a moment, but Sally didn't speak, and so she continued. But as she spoke, the past returned to haunt her and the words seemed only to add emphasis to the memories she was so suddenly reliving.

After an unendurably long winter break, Alison had come back to Stanford. Her first priority had been to call Stephen and tell him she was back. Her second was to get ready to go out with him that night.

During her vacation, she had thought about him endlessly, and knew that she must be in love. She had read a hundred women's magazine articles about love and decided that what they described was what she felt.

She had also read about what was supposed to happen when two people are in love, but that she wasn't so sure about. That night Stephen picked her up, and she reveled in the fact that someone as handsome as Stephen would be with someone like her. She had never been able to fully push aside the picture of herself as she'd been until she had come to college.

It was a wonderful night, and she learned that Stephen had missed her as much as she'd missed him.

Their kisses lasted for a long time, until at last Stephen had drawn away from her and looked deeply into her eyes.

"Alison, I'm not some silly college boy. I can't keep on acting like one."

Alison, feeling a sudden fear that something was wrong, gazed at him with moist eyes. "I . . . I don't understand."

"I'm a man. And I don't like to play games. When two people feel the way we do they need to express themselves."

It took her only a second to understand what he was saying. Doubts rushed through her mind, but easing her doubts were the words he had spoken: "When people feel the way we do . . ." He had said he loved her.

The magazine articles she'd devoured had helped her to understand what he was really saying. And with her nerves screaming, and her stomach turning in circles, she took his hand in hers.

"I understand," she told him in a trembling voice.

A half-hour later, they were in his apartment, and a half-hour after that, Alison Rand was no longer a virgin. But she was in love. She had given herself to him, and although she did not realize that the love-making should have been pleasurable, she did know that she was happy.

As the weeks passed, they made love whenever they were together, and slowly Alison came to the realization that all they ever did anymore was go out for dinner and then return to his apartment. Yet she said nothing, because she believed they were in love.

Not even Lauren Frisch, who was still her room-mate, knew she was dating him. Because he was a professor, and because she didn't want a lot of malicious rumors spreading through the campus, Alison had no one to turn to for advice or guidance, and she let Stephen dictate the terms of their relationship.

Two months after they had become lovers, Stephen's phone calls began to diminish. Whenever Alison asked why, he responded by telling her he was overwhelmed with work.

And then the days came when there were no calls from Stephen anymore. Alison was frantic. She didn't know what to do, and she had no one to talk to.

Resolutely, she walked to his apartment and knocked on his door. Stephen appeared a few moments later, wearing only a bathrobe. "We have to talk," she told him.

"It's a little inconvenient right now," he said.

Alison, unable to believe her ears, felt the start of a new emotion—blind anger. She had trusted him and loved him, and now when she needed him, he was turning her away.

"Now!" she stated. "I need to talk to you now!"

"Please, Alison."

"No," she said, not hearing the strange quality in his voice. "What happened, Stephen? I love you. Why are you treating me this way?"

"Alison," he began, but another voice—a woman's voice—cut him off.

"Who's there, darling? Another one of your students? Can't you tell them you're busy?" With the last word, a ravishingly beautiful dark-haired woman appeared behind Stephen.

He looked at Alison, and then shrugged his shoulders. "Alison Rand, meet Vicki Long, my fiancée. Vicki, Alison is one of my students."

Alison, stunned, stared at the woman and then at Stephen. Slowly, she stepped back, turned and raced away.

"And that's the whole sordid story," Alison said as she withdrew her hand from Sally's.

"Did you report him?" Sally asked.

"Do what?"

"Report him to the school."

"Why? Students and professors date all the time. It's allowed, even if it's not looked on with favor."

"What a bastard!"

"I buried myself deeper in my books, and I was able to get through the rest of the year without going insane. But I did find out a few things."

"Such as?" asked Sally.

"Such as the fact that Stephen Palmer had a reputation as a ladies' man. He liked the innocent students."

"Alison, why didn't you try dating someone else?"

"You said it before. I'm afraid. Sometimes at night, I still think about how stupid and gullible I was."

"But you're not a child anymore."

"I wasn't a child then. But I learned. I learned not to trust a man with my heart."

"No one has ever attracted you like he did?" Sally asked, thinking about the magic that was supposed to be first love.

Alison was silent for a moment as Michael St. Clare's image returned to her. She shook it away as she spoke. "The only dates I went on were the ones you arranged."

"And you hated every moment, didn't you?"

"I didn't hate it. I just wasn't happy. I guess it was

just too much work maintaining my protective shield to be able to enjoy dating."

"Maybe it's time to try and lower that shield."

"Sally," Alison said, shaking her head slowly, ignoring the tears that had stained her cheeks when she'd told the story, "I don't know whether I can lower it."

Chapter Three

Michael negotiated the spiraling curve with ease, and downshifted to second gear as he emerged from the last of the hairpin curve. Smoothly, he accelerated to the legal speed limit, and reached fifth gear as he did. The sound of the car's engine pleasantly filtered in through the open T-roof.

He was driving a prototype car, designed and built by a private firm that had asked him to test it. He had agreed that he would, as a consumer advocate, lend his support to the car if he found the car to be as well built and as safe as the company claimed.

So far, the car was everything the manufacturer promised. It handled like an expensive sports car, was very fuel efficient, and the mechanics who'd gone over the vehicle with a fine tooth comb stated that it was a marvel of engineering.

As far as safety features were concerned, Michael was in full agreement with the manufacturer. Besides a regular seat restraint system, the car was equipped with air bags that inflated instantly upon impact; the bumpers were designed to withstand damage at low speeds.

Michael had been testing the car for a full month, and in another week he would have to give the company his report. If nothing went wrong in the next seven days, he would give the car his highest endorsement. And that was a rare thing.

Michael crested another rise, and stretched his legs. He had been driving for almost four hours, and would reach the Tall Pass Dude Ranch in another fifteen minutes.

What a day, Michael said to himself. It had been a hectic one. From the moment he had walked into his office, he had been deluged with phone calls from various newspapers and television stations. It seemed that his appearance on Dan Marshall's show had caused more interest than Michael had realized or expected.

His manipulations to get a series of debates between him and Alison Rand had been premature. If he'd waited one more day, he would have had the pick of the litter.

There had been three newspaper stories discussing the show and calling for more dialogue between him and Alison. Apparently, their on-camera battle had caught the eye of the community, and support was almost equally divided between them.

One of the most interesting calls had been from the organizers of the annual Computer Programmers and Authors Guild conference, offering him a chance to stand before the assembled masses of computer specialists and discuss the subject of subverting youth through computer games.

He had promised to get back to them.

After that call, Michael had asked Anne to get in touch with Alison's boss at Tri-Tech, and convince him that Alison should continue as their spokesperson.

Anne had done just that. By noon Tri-Tech had reluctantly agreed, knowing that to refuse would hurt their image in the public's eye.

But Allan Worley, the president of Tri-Tech, had also stated that it would be up to Ms. Rand to choose whether to be their spokesperson. If she declined, Tri-Tech would appoint someone else.

Not if I can help it, Michael stated for the twentieth time since Anne had given him the news. Anne had also, by some miracle, learned where Alison was vacationing. An hour after that, Michael had been on the road, smiling to himself; of all the places Alison Rand could have chosen, she had picked the one place where he had an advantage.

Michael slowed the car as he reached the turnoff to the ranch. He had made this trip at least twice a year over the past five years, and felt as if he were coming home.

Six years before, his college roommate, Douglas Carey, had begged and borrowed every last cent he could to buy out an old dude ranch and rebuild it into a luxury resort. The result had been the Tall Pass Dude Ranch, and the money Michael had loaned Douglas had been repaid before the first year of the new operation had ended.

Michael, who had never before ridden a horse or spent any time in the mountains, had fallen in love with the outdoors, and the easy life at the dude ranch. Consequently, he had always taken two separate weekly vacations each year at Tall Pass, and when he returned to work, he always felt like a new man.

His last vacation had been three months before, so when he'd called Doug that afternoon, his friend had been surprised. "I'll explain when I get there. I'll only be staying a few days."

When Anne had offered to contact Alison and discuss the t.v. appearances, Michael had cut her off sharply. He had told her he would speak to her himself, and try to get her to agree.

He smiled to himself as he thought of Anne's expression following his unusual pronouncement. But she had been wise enough to keep her questions to herself. Luckily, there were only a few ongoing projects at present, none of which required his presence.

Michael downshifted as he passed under the wooden trellis entrance of the Tall Pass Dude Ranch. Four minutes later he was standing at the front desk, shaking hands with Douglas Carey.

The dining room of the dude ranch was quaint with atmosphere. Each table had a small lantern that gave off a soft glow. The overhead lights were just bright enough to allow the guests to navigate through the room without tripping over anything. All the guests, except Sally Leigh.

That afternoon, when Sally and Alison had been on a trail ride, Sally had gotten a piece of dirt in her eye. Before she could stop her automatic reaction, she'd rubbed her eye. The contact lens had torn, and her eye had become inflamed.

Although she had another pair of lenses, she would not be able to use them for at least a full day, and had to depend on Alison to guide her around. Sally was extremely nearsighted. She could see perhaps three feet away—if she was lucky. And although not usually vain, she refused to wear glasses.

"Who's looking at us?" Sally asked after their cocktails had been served.

"No one," Alison responded with relish.

"You're really getting even with me, aren't you?"

"Me?" Alison asked innocently as she lifted her drink and took a sip.

"You. I may not be able to see very far, but I can see your fuzzy face!"

"Then look at your menu."

"Is Carl here?" Sally asked, referring to her date of the night before.

Alison glanced around. "Not yet."

"Warn me when he comes," she said.

"Look at your menu," Alison repeated as she put down her drink and lifted hers.

The menu was small, but the choices looked good. Alison decided on a salad and broiled trout, and when she looked up again, she saw that Sally was finally looking over the menu.

Glancing around, Alison took in the dining room and its occupants. It was a well-mixed group of people, most of whom where in their twenties and thirties. There were as many couples as there were single people, and Alison felt relaxed and a part of everything.

But just as she had finished her inspection and started to pick up her drink again, something caught her eye. Looking at the entrance, she saw two men walk inside.

A second later, her body went stiff with tension. She knew she was staring, but could not take her eyes from the sudden apparition that was drawing near.

It can't be! But it was.

Sally, who had just put her menu down, saw Alison's features tighten. "Alison?"

Alison didn't hear her friend as she watched Michael St. Clare, the man who had been haunting her thoughts for two days, walk gracefully across the room.

Sally turned, squinting to try to make out what Alison was looking at, but all she could see was a blur. "Who is it, Alison?" she asked.

Alison tore her eyes away from the unexpected sight and looked at Sally. "Him."

"Him? Carl?"

"No, *him*. The one from the other night."

"The banker?"

"Oh, Sally! The one from the t.v. show. Michael St. Clare." At that, Michael and the man he was with drew near their table. She saw him pause, as if seeing her for the first time. Then, as her heart pounded, he approached the table with a smile on his too well formed mouth.

"This is a pleasant surprise," he said when he reached Alison's table.

Alison, her body vibrating with the sound of his voice, stared expressionlessly up at him. "I wouldn't exactly call it that," she snapped.

Michael seemed to flinch. His smile vanished, but his eyes were filled with their mysterious sparkle. "Are you always angry? Or is this what happens to people who spend their lives with computers?"

Alison held his stare for an endless moment before she was able to break away from his gaze. Grasping for anything that would hide the way she was reacting to him, she glanced at Sally, who was staring up at Michael with wide, but barely focused eyes.

"Sally, this is the . . . ah . . . the gentleman I told you about from the other night. And, I use the word *gentleman* lightly."

"Sally Leigh," she said, introducing herself and casting an accusatory glance at Alison for her sudden lack of manners. "I've heard a lot about you, Mr. St. Clare," Sally said with her usual dazzling smile.

"If it was from Ms. Rand," Michael said with another smile, "I'm sure none of it was very flattering."

"On the contrary, Alison only said she found you to be an admirable opponent," Sally said with a straight face.

Michael's reply was an eloquent uplifting of his eyebrows. Then he turned back to Alison. "I've always heard that the mountains have a way of making people forget their anger. I do hope it has that sort of an effect on you."

Before Alison could retort, Michael spun on his heels and walked back to his friend. Alison watched him, her fury increasing with each step he took to a table ten feet away from her own.

"He's rather good-looking," Sally said.

Alison favored her friend with a withering gaze. "In an egotistical, bigoted way! Besides, you can't see that far."

"When it comes to handsome men, don't bet on it."

Alison shook her head. "Handsome is on the outside. But what's underneath can be very different."

Sally had been studying Alison intently from the moment Michael had come to the table. Although she couldn't see very far, she had been acutely aware of her friend's reaction to the man. Suddenly, as if a bolt of lightning struck her, she understood what was happening.

"You really like him, don't you?"

Alison glared at Sally, and then picked up her menu without speaking. A moment later, the waiter appeared, and although she had lost her appetite, she ordered anyway.

When they were alone again, Alison tried to make herself relax, but her nerves were screaming and her stomach felt as if something were squeezing it relentlessly.

"I despise him," she said at last.

Sally looked at Alison thoughtfully. "You know, when you went on and on while we were driving here yesterday, I just put it off to your being angry at the trick they pulled on you. And this morning, when you saw the article in the paper, about your appearance on the television show, you got so angry I thought your face would stay a permanent shade of crimson. Now I understand why."

"No way!" Alison denied loudly.

Sally shrugged her shoulders. "Whatever you say."

The meal passed with a slowness made evident by Alison's nerves. The fact that whenever she glanced around the room, she found Michael's eyes fixed upon her didn't help either. Although Sally attempted to keep the conversation flowing, Alison, more often than not, did not hear her. She was too lost in her own thoughts and anger, and in the certainty that Michael was always looking at her.

It isn't fair, she said to herself as she demolished the chocolate mousse she'd ordered for dessert. Michael St. Clare had already ruined her life for the past two days; he had no right to keep on doing it.

"Have you seen Carl yet?" Sally asked when she finished her coffee.

"No."

"You're a regular fountain of verbosity tonight," Sally stated dryly.

Alison started to snap back her answer, but stopped herself. "I'm sorry," she said truthfully, "he just makes me mad."

"Then why don't we go and have some fun and forget all about him?" Sally asked.

I wish I could. "All right," Alison agreed.

"Good! I feel like dancing, and I need someone to screen the men for me."

"Oh, Sally . . ." Alison moaned as she shook her head at her smiling friend.

Douglas Carey put down his coffee and watched the two women walk out of the dining room. Then he turned to Michael. "I've done the impossible for you. The hotel's completely filled, and I've found you a bed to sleep on, haven't I?"

Michael looked at Douglas and slowly nodded his head. Douglas had indeed found him a bed, in his own private cabin. "And?"

"And I want a favor in return."

Michael waited.

"The other woman. The one with Alison Rand. I want an introduction."

"You've never been shy," Michael stated.

Douglas shrugged his shoulders. "Don't ask me to explain. Just do this for me."

Michael saw that his friend was very serious. "All right." Then he turned back to the entrance and watched Alison and Sally disappear through it. For several seconds after they were gone, his eyes remained fixed on the doorway.

The music in the Spur, which doubled at night as a disco, was a far cry from what anyone would expect at a dude ranch. The band was not country/western, but a pop-type group that mixed current rock hits with soft ballads. It was a pleasant blend that seemed to suit all the guests equally well.

Alison had chosen a table far enough away from the dance floor to be inconspicuous, yet close enough to be able to watch everything that happened. The first thing she'd seen, when they'd come into the disco, was Sally's date from the previous night, Carl, dancing with another woman.

She'd told Sally, with evident hesitation, but Sally had just laughed. "He's a nice man, but there are others."

Alison, once again found herself envying Sally's capacity for life. And for the next hour, she sat contentedly back and watched the people dancing. As the minutes passed, her tension ebbed, until she finally started to regain her earlier, more relaxed mood.

Even though she had chosen a table away from the mainstream of traffic, a steady stream of men came over and invited them to dance. Alison had danced twice, but Sally had been on the dance floor more than at the table.

When the band had taken a break, and the noise level was lower, Sally had asked Alison to describe all the men who were sitting alone at the bar. But now that the band was back, Alison turned toward it and watched them begin to play.

A few moments later, Alison felt a presence behind her. She really wasn't in the mood to dance and decided to nicely decline this offer. Turning, she gazed up into the sparkling depths of Michael St. Clare's eyes and froze.

From the corner of her eye, she saw that Sally was once again squinting in a vain effort to see. Before she could speak, another man appeared next to Michael. Only then did Michael speak.

"Alison Rand, Sally Leigh, allow me to introduce Douglas Carey."

Alison nodded at the man, and then saw that Sally was staring at him with a very strange intensity.

"Sally," Michael continued, "Douglas would like to dance with you."

Alison watched as Sally, without speaking a word, stood trancelike and waited for Douglas to come to her. With her hand on his arm, Sally followed Douglas to the dance floor. When Alison brought her attention back to Michael, she realized that he had seated himself next to her.

"May I join you?"

"You already have," she replied tersely. "Why did you do that?"

"What? Sit down?"

"No, have your friend dance with Sally."

"Actually, it was his idea."

"Mr. St. Clare—"

"Michael."

"Why are you bothering me?"

"Why are you bothered? After all, it's only a coincidence that we meet again." Even as he said it, he gave himself a mental kick. He had not wanted to lie; he had wanted to be open and honest with her, but she had put him on the defensive, and he wasn't used to that.

Alison intuitively sensed that something wasn't right.

"Are you enjoying yourself?" he asked.

Alison felt her stomach tighten again even as she summoned her defenses. "Why do you ask? Don't you think 'my kind' of person can? Or do you think I should be in the game room?"

"I wondered about that, but I didn't see you with all the other addicts," he said lightly.

Alison restrained her angered response and vacillating emotions. "You mean you actually ventured into the world of video games?" she asked sarcastically.

"I can't get away from them. They're everywhere."

"Then perhaps you'll have to give up your archaic way of thinking."

Michael smiled at that. No matter how angry she got, he realized, she had a wonderful wit. "Or perhaps, you should try to see the world as it really is."

Alison stared at him, her thoughts racing, seeking some means of retaliation, when he unexpectedly covered her hand with his. The instant his hand touched hers, her body reacted. Her skin felt as though a burning brand were pressing into her flesh. Yet she could not find the strength to pull away from his touch.

"Alison, you're on vacation. Why don't you try to forget your profession—and mine—and enjoy yourself."

Alison, her hand afire, gazed steadily into his eyes. Drawing from every ounce of her strength and willpower, she lifted her free hand from the table and covered his. Then slowly, pointedly, she shook her head and lifted his hand from hers and moved it away. When his hand hovered a few inches above an empty spot on the tabletop, she released it. "My profession is part of me."

Michael shrugged. "Does it affect your feet?"

"Excuse me?" Alison asked, unprepared for his question.

"Would you like to dance?" he asked, giving her his fullest smile.

Alison's heart speeded up with the smile. "I'd love to," she said in a sugary sweet voice. Standing, Alison favored Michael with a smile that did not show the way her body was responding to him. She turned from him and walked to the bar, and to the group of single men seated at it. Picking the first man her eyes fell on, she went over to him and asked him to dance.

The man, after quickly appraising her, agreed and led her to the dance floor. When she passed her table, she saw that Michael was grinning broadly, his eyes glowing mischievously; his hands were coming together in a mock, silent applause.

Michael watched Alison until she reached the dance floor. He knew he was only getting what he deserved. He'd been dishonest with her, and he had to accept the results. Then, knowing that any further efforts would meet with the same resistance, Michael stood and left the disco—he needed to think, and the noise level in the Spur was not conducive to thought. *Tomorrow,* he told himself, thinking again about Alison, *will be another day*.

But once outside, he wasn't so sure. He was playing a two-sided hand. On one side, he wanted to prove to the world that computer games were a danger to the youths who played them, destroying their natural inclinations to use their minds and to sharpen their intellect by interacting with each other and their environment.

His strongest desire was to right this wrong. It was a part of the overall obsession he had to make the people—the consumers—aware of the problems of modern living so that those very people could determine for themselves what products and services to use or not use.

Michael knew that his crusading ways were not always well accepted, but nothing had ever been able to change him, and he doubted that anything would.

The other hand he was playing was purely personal. From the moment he had met Alison, he had found himself drawn to her, his passion insurmountable. Whenever he closed his eyes, he could see every last detail of her exquisitely proportioned face.

He wanted far more than a casual relationship. He wanted her to understand what she was doing to those unaware people who played the games she and Tri-Tech designed. Especially to the teenagers who spent every last quarter in the arcades.

But in coming here, he had broken every rule he had ever placed upon himself. He knew it was wrong to get this involved with the opposition. *And,* he reminded himself, *she is the opposition.*

Then, as Michael looked up at the nighttime sky he knew that opposition or not, he was going to be honest with her. He would tell her how he felt, both about her and about what she did for a living, and then . . .

Then what? he asked himself. *I don't want to lose*

her before I get a chance to win her. With those thoughts, Michael turned back to the Spur.

While she had danced, Alison had watched Michael. She'd seen him leave, but instead of feeling elated in her victory, she felt dejected. The dance lasted forever, and when it was over, she thanked her partner and returned to the table just as Sally and Douglas sat down.

Douglas smiled at Alison, and then looked around. "Where's Michael?"

"I haven't the slightest," Alison replied, keeping her voice as level as humanly possible. Then she turned to Sally and saw that her friend's eyes were locked on Douglas's. She could almost feel the air vibrating, and realized that something very special seemed to be happening between Sally and Douglas.

With a shrug that neither saw, Alison stood. "I'm exhausted," she said. "I'm going to sleep. See you around." She waited for Sally to realize she was leaving.

A moment later, Sally looked at Alison. "Where's Michael?"

"I already answered that one. Night, Sally." She turned and left the disco, ignoring the very puzzled expression on Sally's face.

By the time she reached her room, she was as tired as she'd said she was. It had been a long day, and an even longer night. Moving lethargically, Alison undressed, put on the overlarge tee shirt she used to sleep in, and slipped between the covers.

Closing her eyes, she tried to sleep, but even as she felt herself reaching toward that welcomed release, an image blocked her way.

She tried to ignore it, tried to blank her mind, but

Michael's face grew brighter and her heart began to race again. Her eyes snapped open, and her breathing sounded loud in the room.

Sitting up, she remembered her talk with Sally, and her promise to let down her defenses and give a man a chance to make her feel differently about the world.

It can't be him! she told herself. Closing her eyes again, Alison knew that she could no longer deny that she was very, very attracted to Michael.

Alison made herself remember their first meeting and the cruel trick that was foisted upon her. But as she thought of that she also remembered her first sight of Michael, and the way her entire being had responded to him.

It's not fair, she told herself. Alison knew that he despised everything she believed in. That he was her enemy, and that what he was after was her destruction.

A sudden suspicion made her wonder if it were really only a coincidence that he had come here for a vacation at the same time as she. *What else could it be?*

For two days she had been venting her anger on Michael, believing he was responsible for the cruel set-up on the television show. But now she wondered about that, and at last accepted the possibility that it had been the people running the television show who had set her up, and not Michael.

She thought about the newspaper article she'd read that day, and how the reporter had urged further debates between Michael and the computer industry, and Alison in particular. But, with Michael's fierce reputation, and the ever-present power that surrounded him like a suit of armor, she wondered if it would be a wise thing for her to do.

"I have to hate him!" she declared aloud. But when the words faded into silence, she knew how hard that would be. Finally, unable to argue with herself anymore, Alison lay back down and closed her eyes. This time, Michael St. Clare's face did not try to stop her.

As Alison waged her unwinnable battle with herself, Michael returned to the disco, ready to explain himself to Alison. When he stepped into the darkened room, he saw that only Douglas and Sally were at the table, gazing at each other and holding hands.

Then he looked at the couples who were dancing, but did not see Alison among them. Wondering where she was, he walked to the table and sat next to Douglas.

"Can I interrupt?" he asked.

"You are," Douglas replied without taking his eyes from Sally.

"What happened to Alison?" he asked.

"Sleep," Sally said, her eyes never wavering from Douglas.

Realizing that he was intruding on something special, Michael thought about leaving, but remained. "Sally, if you can tear yourself away from my friend for a moment. . . ."

Reluctantly, Sally took a deep breath and tried to relinquish the magical feelings that were engulfing her. From the moment she had met Douglas, she knew he was the one whom she had been waiting for. She had no doubts at all.

Sally smiled at Michael and waited for him to speak.

"I'd like to know more about Alison."

Sally sighed. "You're very blunt."

"One of my less endearing qualities."

"Why do you want to know about Alison?"

"Curiosity," he replied.

Sally shook her head slowly. "Alison Rand is my friend. She's important to me, and she's a very special person. You, on the other hand, represent something that threatens Alison."

"And you call me blunt?" Michael replied, not at all upset by her statement.

"Michael," Sally said, using his first name as if she'd known him for a long time, "Alison is not used to dealing with your type."

"What type is that?" he challenged.

"Experienced. . . . A man of the world."

"She seems to be able to handle herself quite well."

"Let me put it another way," Sally said with a full smile. "Don't play games with her! If you hurt her, Michael, you'll regret the day you ever set eyes on her, or on me."

Michael stared at her for a long moment before he nodded. He stood slowly, his eyes locked with hers. "I have no intention of hurting her," he stated. "And you should try to remember that it's Alison, not I, who deals with games."

Then he looked at Douglas, who was regarding him and Sally with a faintly amused look. "I'll see you later."

"Much later," Douglas replied as his gaze returned to Sally's and both people instantly forgot that Michael had even been there.

Chapter Four

The incessant ring of the telephone startled Alison. Waking up with a groan, Alison reached to the nighttable that separated her bed from Sally's. As she grabbed the receiver she saw that Sally's bed was empty and the bedding was undisturbed.

She wondered what had happened to her friend even as she spoke into the receiver. "Hello."

"Alison, this is Fran."

"Fran . . . what?" she mumbled, trying to figure out why Fran, her boss's secretary, would be calling her.

"Allan asked me to get you. He said it was very important."

"I'm on vacation. Mark can handle it," she replied. Mark was her assistant at Tri-Tech.

"Not this time," Fran said; Alison detected a funny undertone to her words.

"Why?"

"I'm connecting you with Allan," she said, avoiding Alison's question completely.

Alison sighed, wondering what would be so important that the head of the company needed to speak to her at that very moment. Alison knew that the last program she had written and set up, worked flawlessly.

"Alison?" came Allan Worley's jarring fast-paced voice.

"What time is it?"

"Eight o'clock."

"I'm on vacation!"

"I know. Alison, did you have fun the other night when you did that television show?"

A sinking sensation overcame her. She held the receiver tightly and shook her head before she realized he couldn't see her. "No!"

"Really?" Allan replied. He sounded surprised.

"What's going on?" Alison asked.

"Well, you've been invited to spend a week on a talk show to prove the value of computers."

"Allan, I'm a pragmatist, not a publicist," she pleaded as the warning bells sounded in her mind.

"According to the t.v. people, you made a big hit with the audience, and they feel you would be a good spokesman for us."

"No, thank you."

"Alison, it's important. It . . . it would greatly help our image."

"Our image is fine!" she declared.

"Think of your royalties, and Tri-Tech. Alison, we really need you to do this."

"Allan, please."

Then there was silence on the phone.

Alison waited, and waited. "Allan?"

"Yes?"

"Who else will be on the show?"

"What difference does it make?"

"A lot."

"They said that the same consumer advocate you were with the other night would be on the show."

"No!"

"Alison, do me a favor. Just think about it," Allan requested.

Alison sensed there was something more behind what he was saying. "Why me, Allan? What's wrong with Bob Conran, or Sylvia Leeds from publicity?"

"They want you. Alison, it really might hurt our image if you don't do this. Please think about it."

Alison sighed and tried to figure a way out of this, but for the moment, her mind refused to work. "All right, Allan, I'll think about it. But I don't think I'll change my mind."

"Thanks. Oh . . . enjoy your vacation," he added quickly.

"Sure," Alison replied to the already dead line. Before she could hang up, the door opened and Sally came in.

Alison stared at her, looking her friend over from head to foot.

"Are you okay?" she asked as she finished hanging up the phone.

"Won-n-n-derful," Sally exclaimed while she squinted at Alison.

"You didn't sleep here last night."

"Noooo, I didn't."

"Sally. . . . You just met him!"

Sally smiled and crossed the room to stand close enough to see Alison clearly. "Alison, I may have met

Douglas last night, but I've known him all my life. I dreamed about him from the time I was ten."

Alison shook her head sadly. "So you threw yourself at him."

"Not at all. We had a lovely evening."

"Did you get any sleep?" Alison asked, studying Sally's face and not finding a single shred of evidence that her friend was tired.

"Not a drop. We walked the night away. We just held hands and walked and talked until the sun came up. Then," she said with a wicked smile, "we had an early breakfast. Did you know that Douglas owns Tall Pass?"

"I don't think anything can surprise me after the last twelve hours," Alison whispered, doing her best to conceal her relief at Sally's words. "He owns it?"

"Uh-huh."

"Go to sleep Sally."

"Uh-uh. I'm meeting Douglas in an hour. We're going for a ride. Want to come?"

Alison shook her head hopelessly. "No, thanks. Sally . . ."

"Uh-huh?" she replied dreamily.

"Don't let him hurt you."

Sally's laugh caught Alison off guard. She stared at her friend and waited for an explanation.

"Sorry, it wasn't what you said . . . exactly." But Sally could not bring herself to tell Alison about her conversation with Michael and the warning she had issued him the night before on that very subject.

"Who was on the phone? One of the men from last night?" she asked, changing the subject deftly.

"Did you ever find that you were losing control over your life?" Alison replied with her own question.

"Don't get into philosophy this morning."

"Seriously. Have you ever felt that way?"

"Constantly," Sally admitted.

"Well, I haven't, at least not in the last few years!"

"So? You still haven't answered my question."

"I was talking to my boss. He wants me to do more television shows. It seems that I made some sort of a hit."

"That's great!"

"Michael will be on the shows also."

"Oh . . ."

"I told Allan I wouldn't do it," Alison said.

Sally shrugged her shoulders. "Michael is a formidable opponent. He's used to being on television and arguing his case." Sally knew she shouldn't get involved in this, but Alison's strong, uncharacteristic actions where Michael was concerned alluded to her friend's true feelings.

"Yes, he is," Alison agreed.

"And you hate him and everything he stands for."

"Yes! No!" Suddenly Alison wasn't so sure. Sally's words were so final. "I . . . I don't hate him, and I certainly don't hate what he stands for. Michael St. Clare has proven himself over and over that he really does do his best to help the people he's trying to protect." Alison paused to collect her thoughts and try to figure out how she had suddenly become Michael's defender.

"It's just that he's attacking what I stand for, and I don't think it's justified."

"But he does."

"That's the problem."

"Then make him see it from your eyes," Sally suggested.

"It's not that simple!"

"Isn't it?" Sally asked. Sally went to her dresser and started rummaging through it. "I think I can wear my lenses today . . . if I can find them."

Behind her, Alison took a deep breath and tried to sort out the confusion of the past five minutes.

When Michael woke up, he did so without his usual slow rise to consciousness. One minute he was sleeping deeply, the next, he was wide awake.

As he gazed out the open window and watched the rays of the sun filtering through the leaves of the trees, his thoughts once again centered on Alison Rand. He knew that it was the anticipation of seeing her this morning that had awakened him.

Since he'd met her, he'd thought of her in terms of his desires and wants. But he'd consistently refused to delve deeper into the layers of emotions that had preceded those thoughts. Now he was doing just that, and he realized that his feelings were much more than just desire.

Michael had never heavily pondered the reasons why he always gave precedence to his work, instead of the development of a relationship. But now that he thought about it, he understood that he had never sought a lasting relationship with any of the women he'd dated because he had not found a woman whom he could consider his equal. And Michael would never permit himself to settle for anything less.

He had always seemed to date women who were only attracted to him because of the power that he wielded. Usually, by the third date, he had seen through the facades that these women wore. He had seen their lack of a personal goal other than to find a man to marry in whose limelight they could stand.

Michael had dated infrequently over the last two

years. He rarely went out with the same woman more than once and usually only because there was a function he had to attend.

But now Michael was certain that Alison Rand was not that type of woman. He knew that he would do whatever was necessary to make Alison a part of his life, and himself a part of hers.

With those thoughts spurring him on, Michael left the bed, showered, dressed and, all the while, thought of ways to win Alison.

After finishing a light, solitary breakfast, and trying, but failing, not to think of the phone call from her boss, Alison left the dining room and started to wander randomly around the ranch.

Her thoughts had a tortured, unceasing quality to them, and with every step she took, another thought would strike her. When she reached one of the corrals she leaned against its fence, closed her eyes and let her mind free.

She thought about Allan's phone call and wondered about his insistence that she appear on the show. Her loyalty was strong to Tri-Tech; it was the only company she had ever worked for. She had started there after college and had never felt the urge to look elsewhere.

She had been in her last month of college when Allan Worley had recruited her for Tri-Tech, and she'd been excited at the prospect of working for a relatively new company with a small staff. Tri-Tech had fifteen employees, and she would be one of its three software writers. Within days of starting work, Alison had felt like she was part of a family.

Tri-Tech had never been a computer game company, and their annual profits weren't very large. Their work had been primarily in the medical and aerospace fields, which had been one of the things that attracted her. But shortly after she'd started work, the aerospace industry began to suffer setbacks. By and large, Tri-Tech had been forced to survive on the minimal profits from its medical work, which was an important and necessary part of Tri-Tech, but not an area that made very much money.

By the end of her first year, Alison had changed that. She'd written two video games that had been sold to a game manufacturer and had brought Tri-Tech a huge sum of money, and a viable alternative to bankruptcy.

Yet, with all the glamor that had been focused on Tri-Tech and on its game writers, the company continued to write new and better medical programs, and Alison was proud of her contribution.

But why did Allan seem worried? she asked herself as she opened her eyes and looked at the horses in the corral.

Because of the increased demands for more advanced and complicated computer games, Tri-Tech had grown into a large and powerful force in the industry. Still, no matter how large it got, or how much money it put into game development, it always put equal, if not more time and money into the medical projects.

Was that the reason? she asked herself. Then she realized that it had to be. If the income to Tri-Tech dropped, the development of newer and better medical diagnostic programs would also fall by the wayside. Dr. Allan Worley was a good man, and a dedicated research doctor, besides being a c῀ ῀ nuter specialist. He would never let something happen to jeopardize his company. Nor would he, Alison believed, let his own needs push someone to do something he or she did not want to, such as appearing on a television show.

"Why do I have to have such a logical mind?" she asked the spotted horse who had wandered over to her in search of a treat.

The large animal stared at her as if it were pondering the subtleties of her question. Then it snorted.

"I agree," Alison said, smiling and patting the horse on its muzzle.

Reminding herself that she was on vacation, Alison tried to push her problem aside. As she worked to achieve that minor miracle a voice interrupted her.

Before the first syllable died, her chest tightened and her stomach did a flipflop. Turning, she stared into Michael's eyes and, without a word, began to walk away.

She kept her eyes fixed on the dude ranch's central building, while behind her, Michael's footsteps drew closer. Halfway to the building, he reached her side.

"Do you always run away when you're afraid of something?" he asked, his voice as soft as his words were sharp.

"Afraid of what?" Alison challenged, stopping to face him squarely and regretting it the moment she had. His eyes raced across her face, even as his lips formed a smile.

"Me, it seems."

"That's ridiculous," Alison stated, hoping that she had been able to make her voice sound convincing and steady. But the truth of his words struck her forcefully.

"Then walk with me for a little while," he suggested.

"To what purpose? We have nothing in common, Mr. St. Clare."

"Michael, please. Mr. St. Clare was my father. And yes, we do have a lot in common," he told her, refusing to let his smile falter, or to take his eyes from her magical blue ones.

"Mr. . . . Michael," she said at last, giving in on this one point. "I don't know of a single thing that we share."

"We can start with the ground beneath our feet, the air we breathe, the sky overhead. . . ."

His voice was like a soft caress. His words evoked strange responses from her emotions, and his eyes, searching her face, did not lessen the impact of the man himself. She looked at him, trying to sense if he was making fun of her.

"Are you always this . . . esoteric?"

"Only when the need arises," Michael replied, relieved that she had not walked away.

"All right," she said, realizing that she was not giving in to him as much as she was giving in to her own emotions.

They turned together, and Alison let Michael guide her away from the main buildings of the ranch, and outward toward the more open areas.

They walked silently for several minutes, and Alison grew more and more conscious of the way the special air of masculinity that Michael carried with him grew to encompass her as well.

Why am I here with him?" she asked herself. Her mind was already a mass of confused and twisted thoughts. She was being torn in a number of different directions, and at the root of it all was Michael St. Clare, with his handsome face, his sparkling eyes and his ability to scare the hell out of her.

She stopped suddenly. "Why are we walking together?"

"Why not?" he responded.

Alison shook her head and then smiled. "Perhaps you're right. All we have in common is what's around us." She waited for his response and found herself surprised to see him shake his head.

"We have much more in common than that, but it's as good a start as any."

Alison gazed into his hazel eyes, her heart suddenly fluttering, her stomach returning to its irritating new habit of turning upside down. Fighting with all her strength, Alison reined her emotions under control.

"I see no reason to start anything."

Michael stared at her, refusing to accept her statement and wanting to tell her how much she affected him. But he realized that no matter what he said, she would not be able to accept it.

Seeing Michael's face tighten, Alison sensed she had pushed him once too much. But she refused to back down, and matched his stare with her own.

"When I first saw you, I thought you were a very special person. The more I see you, the more I believe that," he said in a low voice.

"I . . ." Alison began, but could not find the words she wanted to say. What he'd just said had been like an attack upon her senses. It frightened her more than any harsh words he could have uttered. "Thank you," she whispered. Then she turned and started away.

"Wait!" Michael called, and seeing that she continued walking he went after her. A moment later, he put a restraining hand on her shoulder.

Alison, feeling the searing heat of his hand through her cotton top, spun to pull free. "I can't!"

"You can't run away from yourself," he said in the same low voice he'd used earlier.

"Can't I?" she asked. But she already knew the answer. Shaking her head slowly, Alison drew her gaze from his. "Why are you here?"

Michael, sensing her emotional upheaval, decided that he could not tell her the entire truth—not yet. "Because you're here," he said.

Alison blinked her eyes several times at this revelation. "Then it wasn't just a coincidence?"

"No. I wanted to see you again. When you walked off the television show, I knew I couldn't let you walk out of my life."

"How did you find me?"

Michael smiled. "That was easy. I have the best research team on the West Coast. But, that's not what's important. What is, is that I found you."

Alison laughed despite the way she felt, and for the moment, the tension that hung so thickly over them was broken. "I like your honesty."

"Most people don't," he told her, his voice steady.

Alison tried to maintain the lightness that her laugh had evoked, but as she looked up into his face, the tension resurfaced.

"It can't work." But her whisper held no confidence.

"It can't hurt to find out."

"Can't it?" she asked as her eyes roamed his face, searching for whatever answers lay beneath the surface.

"I won't let it," he promised. "Please, walk with me." Saying this, he held out his hand.

Slowly, almost reluctantly, Alison reached out her

own hand. She knew that once their hands touched, she would be committed to taking this dangerous, risk-filled chance. But as she continued to gaze at him, and felt the way her heart was crying out, she put her hand in his.

"Do I look all right?" Alison asked as she stood before Sally.

She was wearing a simple wrap-around dress that lent an image of height to her body, while accenting her smooth curves to perfection. The straps of the dress were tied behind her neck, and the uneven handkerchief-style hem displayed random flashes of her calves.

Leather sandals adorned her feet; her hair was brushed straight back from her face. Alison's makeup was light, with only a hint of blue shadow on her lids, and a delicate crimson on her lips. A subtle line of mascara around her eyes made them look even larger than they were.

"Lovely," Sally told her approvingly.

"Sally, I'm nervous."

"Don't be. You already took the first step, didn't you?"

"Literally," Alison replied with a hesitant smile. She and Michael had walked for almost an hour. Their conversation had been light, purposefully kept that way by both of them. When they'd returned to the main building of the ranch, Michael had turned to her, his face set in serious lines.

"Will you have dinner with me?" he'd asked.

Without realizing it, Alison had nodded her head.

"Then I'll see you at seven." And then he was gone. For the rest of the day, Alison had walked about, watching the other guests enjoying themselves, and gazing at the couples who were riding, swimming and having a good time.

When she'd returned to her room after lunch, to change into her bathing suit, she'd found Sally sound asleep. Rather than wake her, Alison had changed and gone to the pool. An hour later, Sally had joined her there.

Sitting at the pool, she'd told Sally about what had happened that morning, and about her date that night with Michael. All Sally had done was smile and suggest that Alison and Michael join them at dinner.

Alison, her heart filling with gratitude, had thanked Sally.

"Alison?" Sally said for the second time.

Alison quickly shook away the memory of the day. "Sorry. What?"

"Have you thought any further about doing the t.v. shows?"

"A lot further. But I still don't know," she admitted with a shrug.

"Well, don't let anyone make up your mind for you. Do what you think is best," Sally advised as she stood. "Ready?"

"No," Alison answered as she picked up her small clutch and followed Sally out of the room.

Alison stepped into the cool night air a half-step ahead of Michael. The sky was clear, and the stars dotted the heavens with breathtaking brilliance.

They had lingered over dinner for three hours. At first, Alison's nerves had jangled madly, resounding with the echo of her first sight of Michael as he and Douglas walked into the lounge.

Michael had strode purposefully toward them, his handsome face wreathed with a smile. The deep grooves of crow's-feet spreading out from the corners of his eyes had taken her breath away.

His strong chin and well-defined features had attacked her senses relentlessly, and as he'd drawn closer her heart started to race madly. The aura of electricity that surrounded him seemed to become amplified, and his graceful walk had turned leonine.

When he'd reached her and taken her hand to lead her into the dining room, she'd felt little shocks race along her skin from his touch. But as the evening progressed, she'd been able to relax and enjoy herself and the three people she was with.

"Thank you," Michael said when he came abreast of Alison and looked down at her.

"For what?" she asked, puzzled, tilting her head so she could gaze up at him.

"For having dinner with me tonight."

Alison didn't know what to say. Instead, she shrugged her bare shoulders and started to walk again. The silence that descended remained until they reached the same corral where they had met that morning.

When they were by the fence, Michael reached out and turned her toward him. He looked directly into her eyes, and the muscles in his hands, feeling the softness of the bare skin of her shoulders, tightened.

"Alison," he began in a husky voice.

Alison, overly aware of how wonderful his hands felt on her skin, saw a change come over his face. When he spoke her name, her entire being reacted to him. Suddenly, she knew he was going to kiss her, and her fears returned.

"Please, Michael," she whispered, shaking her head and stepping back, trying to escape from both him and herself. But his hands tightened securely on her shoulders, and his strength stopped her from the escape she so desperately sought.

Unable to prevent it, she was drawn into his embrace. His arms went around her, imprisoning her tighter than any bars could. As she stared up at him, his mouth slowly descended toward hers.

Their lips met and her body stiffened. While she fought against what was happening, her body was surrendering to him. His lips were as demanding as they were pliant; his arms were like steel bands. Unknown emotions rose within her, shaking her to her very core as the kiss deepened into a passionate, all-consuming fire that threatened to rob her of her sanity.

His strong, muscular body pressed to hers, and it felt as if neither of them wore clothing. Against her will, her lips softened, yielding to his unspoken demands. Her mind spun, and within her, she felt the birth of desires to which she'd never believed herself susceptible.

The kiss seemed to last for an eternity, tearing her away from the real world and bringing her to a strange place that she did not know existed. In that unchartered region, her mind began to operate again, and from deep within it came a scream of fear that jarred her back to sanity.

When the kiss ended, and Michael's arms loosened but did not release her, she was able to slow the confused whirling of her mind and control the painful pace of her heart.

She stared defiantly at him and saw that he was breathing as hard as she. "Don't do that again!" she commanded, quickly pulling free from his arms.

"I won't promise not to kiss you again, and I won't apologize for something we both wanted to happen," Michael stated, his eyes never wavering from hers.

Alison's sharp intake of breath was loud in the night. She shook her head in denial. "Don't let your ego decide what I want to do!" Then, with her heart once again pounding, she stalked away from him toward the direction of her room.

Behind her, Michael stood still as she disappeared into the night. Although he ached to go after her, he knew that now was not the time. From her reaction to his kiss, it was obvious that no matter what she said, or how fervently she denied it, her emotions matched his own.

Just then Sally and Douglas walked over to him. "Where's Alison?" Douglas asked.

Michael shrugged. "She went back to her room."

"Another fight?" Sally fixed Michael with a penetrating stare.

"You might say that."

"Michael," Sally began in a thoughtful voice, again aware that she should not interfere in the lives of Alison and Michael, but unable to stop herself because of her concern and love for her friend, "Alison isn't a run-of-the-mill person. You have to be patient, and you have to accept her for who she is."

Michael shook his head slowly, his mouth still set in a firm line. "I can accept her for who she is. I'm even willing to accept her for what her career is. What I can't accept is the fact that every time we're together, somehow she ends up stalking away and I stare at her back!"

"Give her time," Sally advised.

Michael thought about that, and about the manipulations he'd already put into progress—manipulations that she would sooner or later find out about. Intuitively, he knew that if he didn't break down some of her barriers soon, they would become true adversaries.

"I don't have time."

Chapter Five

Alison stared at the ceiling, wondering why her sleep had been so poor. She remembered awakening and glancing at the clock when Sally returned to the room. It had been almost four in the morning.

She had fallen back into a fitful sleep, but when the sun rose, so did she. She'd been lying in bed for almost an hour now, trying to sort out the confusing mix of her emotions.

On one hand she knew she had to hate Michael St. Clare, because of what he was trying to do. She had known of him for several years, and of his crusades to protect the buying public. She had read many of his articles, and in college had followed his column in the local paper whenever she had a chance.

The one thing that she was certain of from her previous knowledge of Michael St. Clare was that once he set his mind on a goal, he pursued it relentlessly until he had conquered it and exposed it for what it was.

She remembered one particularly vivid account of his crusade against a candy manufacturer that Michael had believed was using a cancer-producing agent in its products. The media had widely publicized the battle that had raged for six months, as Michael fought both the manufacturer, and the Food and Drug Administration at the same time. The results, Alison had read, had driven the manufacturer out of business.

Michael and his organization had proven that the additive—which had been considered a harmless preservative—was indeed a strong carcinogenic.

Alison shuddered. After meeting Michael in the flesh, she sensed that he was the type of man who, once he made up his mind to go after something, would pursue it ruthlessly. If he was after the computer industry, just the publicity of his name alone would be enough to alienate a vast number of consumers.

But why is he really at the ranch? she asked herself. It was a question that had been hovering over her since she'd seen him in the dining room. *Is he trying, in some way, to undermine me?* But Alison dismissed the thought.

Her emotions rose to do battle with the logic that had centered her thoughts on Michael's past doings. She wanted to be wary of him and not to think of him as anything other than the enemy; but her heart refused to heed her pleas.

Looking over at the peacefully sleeping face of her closest friend, Alison finally admitted that her fears were not of Michael St. Clare, the consumer advocate, but of Michael St. Clare, the man.

Denying how she felt was no longer working. The

memory of last night's torrid kiss was more than just a haunting memory. Even on this new day, their one kiss was still reflected in her emotional turmoil; it left her no choice but to admit her attraction to him.

No! It's more than just an attraction. Three and a half years ago Alison had decided that she would never be hurt again. She had succeeded in protecting herself very well—until Michael had come into her life.

After her disastrous love affair with Stephen, she had doubted her capacity to love again, and even questioned what love was. But with her newly discovered desires rising to taunt her, she again wondered about the vagaries of that emotion called love.

Can I love? she asked herself. *Do I want to take so big a gamble?* She tried to say no, fought the answering surge of her heart . . . and lost.

Alison tried using the reassuring coolness of logic; her common sense told her that she must not let him suspect how quickly he was winning her heart. Before she could commit herself, she had to be certain that he felt the same emotions as she, and that she was not merely the focus of one of his crusades. She did not want to be fought for, won and then left on the battlefield, shattered by her emotions and his desires.

Again the powerful memory of last night's kiss rose in her mind. Alison's body responded as if he were holding her right then, and kissing her so ardently that she might faint.

"No!" she declared, sitting up and throwing off the covers.

"What?" Sally asked, blinking sleep from her eyes.

"Nothing."

"Good," Sally stated as she closed her eyes and fell back asleep.

Why can't I be more like you? Alison asked silently as she looked at her sleeping roommate.

Michael hung up the phone and stared at the ceiling. He'd been up since six, sorting out his feelings for Alison. By seven, he had figured out nothing, and by eight, he picked up the phone and called Anne Harding at home.

She'd answered on the second ring, and it was clear from the sound of her voice that she'd been awake for a while.

After the amenities, Michael got down to business. "Have I missed anything?"

"Nothing," Anne had responded. "Everything is status quo. Oh . . . I spoke with John Lawson. He said that he's scheduled the first debate between you and Alison Rand for a week from Monday."

Michael had remained silent while he digested this latest piece of information. Before he said anything, Anne had continued. "The man who runs that computer conference called again. He says he needs an answer. I gave him a tentative yes. By the way Michael, you have gotten Ms. Rand to agree to do the show, haven't you?"

"I'm working on it," he'd said in a coarser voice than he'd intended.

"Is there a problem?" she'd asked.

"Nothing I can't handle."

"Well, I've already given you a little hand in that department."

Michael sensed danger. "What is that supposed to mean?"

"After you left, I called Tri-Tech and spoke with Allan Worley. I suggested that he make sure that Ms.

Rand be the Tri-Tech representative to debate you, or that you might target Tri-Tech very, very heavily."

Michael had sat back after Anne had spoken and tried to understand why she had gone to that extreme. He had been unable to think of a single reason.

"Why, Anne?" He had tried to keep his voice calm, but he knew the clipped way he spoke imparted his anger. He'd heard Anne's hesitation on the other end and waited.

"I thought you wanted to make sure she was your opponent. Michael, you were the one who started this. You were the one who wanted a television set-up with her!"

Anne's defensive statements had jarred Michael back to his senses. "You're right Anne, you were only doing your job," he admitted truthfully.

The fact was that, on several occasions, he had condoned the very method she had used. At times, and there had been many, Michael needed his opposition to face him in public, and the only way to get them to do so, was to come as close to blackmail as possible. Anne had only been trying to help him, and he understood that completely. But in the past, those other targets had been corporations that were attempting to hide damaging evidence from the public.

Tri-Tech was only one of a large group that, as a whole, was not aware of the potential harm of video games. He only wanted to show them the results of their work, not terrify them into submission.

"I'd like you to call Dr. Worley, apologize in my name, and tell him that we agree to the original terms. It will be Ms. Rand's decision."

"All right, Michael. And . . . I'm sorry."

"It was a simple mistake. No harm was done," he'd said as he hung up. *I hope.*

A few minutes after the phone call, Michael stood, stretched and left Doug's apartment. He needed to get outside for a while. A ride on one of the mountain trails would do just fine, he decided. Perhaps then he would be able to organize his thoughts.

Alison waited patiently for the stable hand to bring out her horse. She had eaten breakfast and had tried to banish the persistent image and the accompanying thoughts of Michael while she ate.

When she'd finished and seen how clear the sky was, she decided to go for a ride. At the stable, she'd learned that the first trail ride would not begin until nine o'clock—an hour from then.

When she'd asked to take a horse out by herself, the man in charge of the stable had explained the ranch's policy. For safety reasons, riders were not permitted to ride alone. At least two people had to go out together.

"There's always someone who likes to take a morning ride. I'll get you a horse, and by then I'm sure there'll be another rider," the stable hand assured her.

While she waited for the horse, she gazed around the ranch, which was just starting to come to life. Behind her she heard footsteps approaching and turned to see if it was a guest in search of a riding partner. The smile froze on her lips the instant she saw who it was.

"Good morning, Alison," Michael said pleasantly, covering his surprise at finding her at the stable.

"Good morning," she replied stiffly.

"Are you going for a ride?"

Alison nodded.

"May I join you?"

She stared at him. "You never give up, do you?"

"Not when it's this important." He paused for a moment, waiting for her tense reaction to ease. "Alison," he said, his tongue caressing the name much in the way he wanted to caress the woman herself, "I know we've fought almost every time we've been together. But something is happening between us, something nice. I don't want to ignore it, and I don't think you do either."

Feeling as though he'd read her mind, Alison took a hesitant breath. Sensing that he was being truthful, she slowly nodded.

"Could we try something?"

"I'm willing," Michael replied immediately.

"Let's learn about each other, not rely on what we think we already know."

"I'd like that," Michael agreed.

A moment later the stable hand came out leading two horses. When he saw Michael standing with Alison, he smiled at Michael but spoke to Alison.

"I thought I might as well saddle two. I guess I was right."

They had been riding for almost an hour, enjoying the day, the views, and the sense of freedom from civilization that horseback riding in the mountains gave them. Their conversation had been infrequent; they were riding one behind the other because of the narrowness of the bridle trail.

"Shall we take a break?" Michael asked when they reached a plateaulike spot on the mountain.

"Fine," Alison responded, looking out into the distance at a second chain of mountains to the east.

After dismounting, Alison and Michael led the

horses to a slender tree and secured the reins to its trunk.

Then Michael pointed toward the mountains Alison had just looked at. "They're on the California, Nevada border. Lake Tahoe is on the other side."

"They're gorgeous."

"But not a match for you."

"I don't ever remember being compared to a mountain before," Alison said with a soft lilt in her voice. Although she had been filled with tension at the beginning of the ride, she was much more at ease now.

"Comparisons of beauty don't have to be restricted to a likeness between the same views."

Alison stared at him for a long second before she laughed aloud, the last threads of her anxiety slipping away. Michael, after pausing a moment to silently repeat the statement to himself, followed suit.

"Did I really say that?" he asked when he controlled his laughter.

"I'll pretend you didn't."

"Good."

"Michael," Alison said, her voice warm and friendly, "what do you do to relax?" As she spoke, she tried not to see the powerful aura surrounding him; she looked at the man himself.

Michael shrugged. "I don't, except when I take my vacations."

"You don't relax?"

He looked out at the horizon. When he spoke, his voice was distant. "My work is my life. It's not the kind of work that you can put aside at the end of the day. When I do what I do best, I do it all the time."

"That's known as being a workaholic."

"No, that's known as being Michael St. Clare." He turned to face her, his eyes impassioned. "Whatever I do, I do it with all my abilities. I put everything I have within me into it, and I see it through to the very end. Sometimes it gets away from me and I lose sight of things around me, but that's the way I am."

Alison watched him as he spoke from the heart, and continued to watch him for several moments after he had finished.

"But how does it affect the people around you?"

"They either accept it or they don't."

"There's no in-between? No middle ground?"

Michael studied her face as he thought about her question. "There's never been a reason for me to have to find a middle ground." Then he smiled. "Enough about me. What about you? What do you do to relax?"

Alison shrugged. "If I'm at the office, I go home and work. If I'm working at home, I just keep working."

"That sounds familiar."

"But I know I'm a workaholic."

Michael's eyes flickered and then intensified into a piercing gaze. "Are you?"

Feeling a flush start at his unexpected insight, she turned to look back down the mountain trail. "Yes. Michael, why do you hate computers?"

"I don't."

She turned back to face him. "Then why are you on this vendetta?"

"I'm not on a vendetta, I'm courting a woman."

Flustered again, Alison took a deep breath. "You know what I mean. Why are you fighting against the computer industry."

"It's not the industry as a whole. Just one segment of it—the games."

Holding back a prick of irritation Alison maintained her calm. "Michael, you're an intelligent man. Surely you can see that you're overreacting."

"No, I can't, because I don't believe I am overreacting."

Alison shook her head, trying to think of a way to make him see his mistake. Before she could say anything else, he spoke.

"We agreed to keep this time together friendly. Let's find another subject."

Reluctantly, Alison agreed, feeling yet another change settle over them. The day was just beginning to grow warm, and the air held the pleasant scent of pine trees mixed with morning dew. Turning, Alison looked at the mountains again.

"Why consumer advocacy?" Alison asked.

Michael gazed at her slender back, taking in the delicate curves. At the exact center of the nape of her neck, her blond hair sparkled under the morning sun. Her checked shirt was tucked into well-fitting jeans that flared smoothly over her hips. His blood heated and his desire for her grew stronger, but he willed an iron control over his body even as he answered her.

"It began in college, where I felt like a sheep being led about without any choices. I . . . we were all told what to buy, where to buy it and how much to spend. It was as if big business controlled everything and left no alternatives."

"There had to be more than just that," Alison said, returning her gaze to his face as she sensed that Michael was reluctant to talk about himself.

"There was," Michael said, thinking back over the years to the beginning. "Douglas Carey was one of my two roommates in college. Greg Milton was another. Only Doug and I graduated." When he paused again, he saw that Alison's eyes were fixed on him, and her features were a study of attentiveness.

"As a high school graduation present, my parents gave me a new car—one that was advertised as an achievement in modern engineering—a safe car. The first year of college was uneventful, but in the middle of the second year, Greg, Doug and I had decided to spend a long weekend in the mountains.

"Friday morning came, and just as I was packing, I received a call from home. My father was in the hospital. I left immediately. But I didn't want to spoil the weekend for my friends, so I loaned them my car and flew home."

Alison felt herself breathing shallowly. Michael's voice had deepened with raw emotions while he spoke.

"My father had had a minor heart attack. But he was okay. The doctors said he would live a long life if he quit smoking and learned to relax a little." Michael smiled briefly. "He quit, and he's still going strong. But on Saturday night, after we got home from the hospital, I got a phone call from the Colorado State Police."

"It seemed there was an accident involving my car. The driver had been killed; his passenger was in the hospital."

"Oh, no . . ." Alison whispered, feeling and sharing the pain that she knew Michael relived daily. Without realizing it, her heart had gone out to him.

"I flew back, rented a car and went to the hospital

where Doug was. He was all right, except for a concussion. But Greg was dead."

Michael drew in a deep breath and then forced himself to go on. "I had spoken to the police before I saw Doug, and they had determined that the brakes had given out on a tight turn. Either they had not been serviced properly, the trooper told me, or Greg had abused them while he drove.

"I didn't want to accept the last part, because I knew Greg was a good driver. When I saw Doug in the hospital, I told him what the police had said.

" 'No!' Doug had yelled. I waited until Doug was ready to talk, then I listened intently. He said that Greg's driving was fine, but the brakes had blown. They had been on a steep decline, and as Greg had pressed on the brakes to slow the car for a turn, they'd heard a loud pop.

"A second later, their speed increased, and Greg had told Doug that the brakes had blown. Then he'd tried to maneuver the car, but the turn came too soon. Halfway through the curve, Greg lost control of the car. It hit the shoulder and flipped over into a stand of trees.

"Greg had been thrown from the car, and died when he struck a tree. Douglas had been luckier. He hit his head on the dashboard and was knocked out.

"When I left the hospital, I went to the auto wreckers to look at the car that had killed one friend and hurt another. I'd spent three summers during high school working in a gas station. What knowledge I'd gained there, I put to use. The car was a mess. Badly crushed and twisted. The first thing I realized was that the hood was still attached, and it was closed."

"I tried to open it, but it wouldn't budge. In that moment, I knew something was very wrong. I knew the police had not inspected the car as they had said. I got a crowbar and popped the hood. When I looked at the master brake cylinder, I couldn't believe my eyes. The entire front of it was missing.

"At first I thought it was a result of the accident, but I was also remembering what Doug had said. I looked deeper and found the fluid line and the piece of the cylinder that was missing. I studied it and saw the ragged edges of a rubber seal. When I touched it, the rubber dissolved in my fingers.

"I wasn't sure what to do, but I knew that it should have been I who was in the car, not Greg. When I spoke to the insurance company, they said that they were satisfied with the police report and left it at that. The insurance adjuster scoffed at my idea that there had been something wrong with the car. 'College kids are known for their irresponsibility when it comes to drinking and driving. Besides,' he added, 'that automobile is the safest in the world.'

"'Then why is my friend dead!' I screamed at him. From that minute on, I was determined to find out what had happened. I brought the piece of the brake cylinder and gasket to the chemistry department and had it analyzed. While they did that, I went to the motor vehicle bureau in Denver and began to research any and all accidents, looking for those that involved the make and model of my car.

"I had been prepared for a long search, but I had hardly started when I began to find reports of accidents involving not only the car, but the same brake problem.

"I spent three solid days looking in the files. I read

two thousand reports. Out of those, I found seven incidents that matched. When I got back to school, the results of the analysis were ready."

Michael paused to take a deep breath and to dispel the ghosts. Then he smiled at Alison, but the smile held no trace of humor. "It seems that the rubber in the gaskets had been mixed with a new type of vinyl to reinforce and lengthen the gaskets' life. It worked fine, for anywhere from twelve to fifteen months, and then suddenly it decomposed.

"The chemistry professor who had analyzed it said he had talked with one of the researchers who had been involved in the early stages of production. The researcher had been unaware of any problem; he had thought the gasket was holding up fine.

"I went to the papers and gave them the results of my findings, sure that they would know a good story when they saw it. Boy, was I in for a surprise. After presenting all the facts to the editor, he shook his head. 'We need proof, not conjecture.'

"I thought I had all the proof he needed. He didn't agree. It wasn't until later that I understood the fine line between newspaper reporting and advertising revenue.

"When Doug got out of the hospital, I told him what we found, and together, with the help of a few more friends, we began to gather all sorts of information."

Michael stopped. "I could go on for a long time," he told Alison.

"For as long as it takes," she said, unwilling for him to stop. It wasn't just a story to her. She was learning more about Michael while he talked than she could possibly learn in any other way. "Please."

Michael sighed gently. "I ended up dropping out of school for that semester, and spent four months traveling around the country. When I was finished, I had enough solid proof to bring to a large paper. One big enough not to be threatened by its advertisers.

"I had five cartons of duplicated accident reports, and the sworn affidavit of the service manager of a dealership. When I walked into the *New York Times,* I went directly to the managing editor, and before he could protest, I handed him the affidavit and told him my story.

"It seems that the manufacturer was aware of the defect, but because the management was afraid of what the publicity would do to sales, they kept the defect a secret. Instead, they had notified their dealerships that whenever that particular model car came in for service, the dealership was to replace the master cylinder. The customer didn't have to know about it."

"Oh, my God," Alison whispered.

"Eight people died in accidents caused by brake failure, and hundreds of others had been seriously injured. The editor sat with me for almost fourteen hours while his staff compiled my documentation and got ready to report my discoveries.

"The end result was that the manufacturer admitted the deception, recalled all the cars and offered a public apology."

"It should have been shut down!" Alison stated angrily.

"It almost was. The lawsuits that were thrown at it almost bankrupted the company."

"You must have felt a great sense of achievement," Alison said.

Michael shrugged. "Not really. What I discovered,

after it was all over with and I had time to think logically, was that the automobile manufacturer hadn't really believed itself guilty of any wrongdoing. It was just following a pattern that had become a part of our overall social structure."

Alison nodded thoughtfully as she contemplated her new insights of Michael. She realized, to a degree, why Michael did so many of the things he did, taking on not just the corporations, but the attitudes of the people themselves.

"Did you go back to school after that? Or did your career start then?" Alison asked.

"I went back to school. I had asked the papers not to identify me. I had done what I set out to do, I had avenged my friend's death. But when I was back in school, I started thinking about all the other things that might happen to unwary people. I continued to study sociology, but every elective I took was in another field. Engineering, education . . . whatever I thought would help me for what I intended to do."

"Become a consumer advocate."

"No, that word wasn't really in fashion then. All I knew was that I didn't want anyone else losing a friend the way I did. I wanted to make sure I could do whatever was possible to achieve that end. It's that simple."

"No," Alison stated with a quick shake of her head. "You're not that simple, Michael St. Clare."

"Enough of the past," he commanded. "We're in the present now and I want to enjoy it with you."

Alison closed her eyes for a moment. She had been drained by his story, saddened at his loss, but better able to understand the passions behind his motivations. When she opened her eyes, she saw he was staring at her.

"That would be very nice," she whispered.

"Michael seemed so different. It was as if I was with another person," Alison said to Sally.

"Isn't it nice to let your defenses down?" Sally asked.

Alison nodded slowly. "But not all of them," she whispered.

"Alison, I'm the last person in the world to give advice. I mean, my track record hasn't been too good . . . until now. And I do know how frightening it can be to open yourself up to a man and trust him with your emotions. But like I said before, if you don't take a chance, you'll never know what could have been."

"I'm starting to understand that, I think," Alison began, watching Sally as she packed one small suitcase. "Can I ask you a question?"

Sally paused as she looked at a nightgown. "Ask."

"Where are you going?" Alison had returned to the hotel room ten minutes before, and as she had talked to Sally about the hours she'd spent with Michael she watched Sally take out the suitcase and start to pack it.

"To meet Mom and Dad."

"To what?" Alison asked, her words echoing the surprise she felt. "They live in Maine."

"Not mine, Douglas's."

"Douglas's . . . Why?"

Sally stopped what she was doing and walked over to where Alison sat on her bed. Lowering herself down next to her, Sally looked directly into her friend's eyes.

"It's the accepted thing to do before people get married."

"I know tha—"

"Take that silly look off your face!" Sally ordered sternly.

"Two days, Sally. You've only known him for two days."

"It doesn't matter. I know him, and I know myself."

"Oh, Sally. Don't rush like this. Please slow down. Think about what you're doing. What if it's a mistake? You could be ruining your life."

"Or I could be happy for the rest of it too." As Alison readied another salvo, Sally held up her hand. "Don't do this to me, Alison. I'm in love with Douglas. I feel it with every part of my being. And I won't allow myself to think it won't work. It will, because we'll make it work!"

Alison read the conviction in Sally's eyes and did not have the heart to dampen her friend's spirits. But neither could she find anything to say.

"Alison, don't take what I have to say the wrong way, please." Sally waited until Alison nodded her head before continuing. "I take risks. I'm willing to take a chance that will make me a happy person. I also think it's about time you came out of the turtle's shell you've wrapped yourself in and face the real world. And I don't mean to take a quick look and sneak back inside. Come all the way out."

"You mean take a chance with Michael?" Alison asked after she recovered from Sally's words.

"No. I don't mean Michael specifically. I mean

anyone. Try to live, not just exist. . . . Oh, Alison, I'm sorry. I'm nervous about meeting Doug's folks, and what I'm saying is coming out all wrong."

"No, it's not," Alison whispered. "It's coming out all right."

The hardest part to accept was the fact that she was speaking only the truth. "Sally, I don't know which is more frightening. The thought of being alone for the rest of my life, or of trusting someone again."

Sally took Alison's hand in her own. "I can't help you make any decisions, and I don't know if you want me to. What I can do is be your friend and accept whatever choice you make."

Alison bobbed her head, afraid to trust words at that moment. Her emotions were verging on running away, and she didn't want to cry. "Finish packing," she said at last.

Sally smiled and stood. "Maybe I should ask Douglas to hold off for a few days before we—"

"Not if it's because of me. If you want to think about the future for a few more days . . ."

"I've thought about my future," Sally said in a level, serious voice. "And life with Douglas is that future."

"Then go tonight," Alison told her.

"Yes, ma'am! But do me a favor?"

Alison arched her eyebrows.

"Think about what you have now, and what you really want out of life."

Alison exhaled slowly. "That's all I've been doing for the last two days," Alison admitted to her friend.

Chapter Six

With every hour that passed, Michael knew he was losing more and more of his heart to Alison. Throughout dinner he had watched her, studied her and talked with her. He didn't know whether she had a natural ability to draw conversation from him, or if he just enjoyed talking with her. But which ever it was, he'd responded fully.

After dinner they had gone to the disco, found a small table off to one side, which, miraculously, was, nowhere near any of the loudspeakers that poured music into the room.

They had danced every slow romantic dance that was played, and he had luxuriated in the feel of his hands on her. She had worn a summer dress that had been held up by two thin shoulder straps. It dipped low on her back and fitted her slender curves to perfection.

The warmth of her body against his had been a

constant reminder of how much he wanted her, but he had kept his desires under control throughout the night.

Although she had seemed relaxed, Michael knew that there were things bothering her. He had felt the low-lying tension in her muscles and had sensed the strain behind her voice and in the looks she had favored him with.

He had also known, that tonight, somehow, he would make her understand how he felt, and tell her too that he did not want to have her for an enemy. But each time he had begun to say something about them, Alison had changed the subject as quickly as possible.

He had not forced his words on her and had accepted things for the moment, but as the night went on, he knew he could not wait much longer.

Pushing aside his thoughts, he gazed at her in the dimly lit room as the driving, fast rock-beat faded away. Then the band's singer made an announcement. "Last dance," he said smoothly into the microphone. The band struck a slow, undulating chord.

Without a word, Michael rose to his full height and offered Alison his hand. Standing, she smiled at him and put her hand in his. But instead of going to the dance floor, Michael led her out of the disco and into the night. The music reached out to them, lower, softer, but still danceable. He took her in his arms, held her close and began to move with the rhythm.

Unable to resist the lure of the music, the illumination of the moon and the blanket of stars, Alison swayed against Michael's lean, powerful body.

They danced slowly, magically, in the night, until the sounds of the music died, and the guests filtered out of the disco.

"That was lovely," Alison said in a husky whisper, afraid that he would notice that her voice was shaking.

"It was," he agreed. Still holding her hand, he began to walk, having no destination in mind. A few minutes later, he stopped to look at her again.

"Alison," he began, only to feel her hand stiffen in his.

Alison had intuitively known that throughout the night, Michael was trying to say things to her she had not wanted to hear. Each time he had, she'd found a way to change the conversation, but now she knew it would be impossible.

"Did Douglas tell you?" she asked.

"Yes. I think it's terrific."

"Do you? Don't you think it's impulsive to talk about marriage after knowing someone for only two days?"

Michael smiled. "I've known Doug for almost fourteen years. He's far from impulsive."

"Exactly what would you call his actions?"

"Making himself happy. Accepting his fortune at finding someone whom he wants to spend his life with." As he spoke, he watched Alison's reactions closely.

"How can he be certain that it will work out?"

Then Michael understood. He shook his head slowly and captured her other hand with his. His eyes locked with hers, and his voice was low but filled with power.

"He can't be certain. Neither can Sally. All they can do is give enough of themselves to make it work. What they can't be is afraid of each other or of themselves."

Alison took a deep breath. She felt as though she

were falling into the bottomless depths of his eyes. Her body cried for her to leap within them, but her mind refused to grant her that freedom.

"But they need to learn about each other. They need time to adjust to each other's ways and moods," she protested.

"They will, together," Michael stated.

"I . . ."

"Alison, don't project your own fears onto Doug and Sally. They know what they're doing. It doesn't frighten them. They may be nervous because they're about to take a very big step, but they aren't frightened of each other. If they were, they would be here tonight, not a hundred and fifty miles away."

Alison did not want to hear his remonstration, but she couldn't help herself either. She shook her head slowly as Michael released her hands and then raised his to cup her face.

Warmth radiated where his hands touched her. Her body tensed, her mind spun madly. She could not speak or move.

"Don't be afraid—not of me, not of yourself. I've already told you that I think you're special. Alison, I've wanted you from the moment I saw you. I can't even begin to tell you how much."

Slowly, Michael lowered his mouth to hers without releasing her face. His lips were not demanding; they felt like gentle flutters of butterfly wings across her mouth.

Alison, standing tautly, felt the warmth of his mouth on hers. She did not try to pull away, nor did she allow herself to respond to his kiss. But without realizing it, the tenderness of his lips began to break down her resistance.

Suddenly his lips left hers, his hands dropped to her shoulders. "You feel it too."

Alison's eyes roamed the contours of his face. Her arm seemed to rise of its own volition. Her fingertips gently traced the outline of his face. Silence continued to reign supreme as her hand gently stroked his cheek.

Michael forced an iron control over himself, knowing that to move would frighten her away. But when she started to lower her hand, he caught it and brought it to his lips. Gently, slowly, he kissed the back of her hand. Then he turned it over and lavished her soft palm with a slow, lingering caress from his lips.

Alison's heart stopped when he brought her hand to his mouth; when he turned it over and branded her palm, it started to beat again, wildly—madly. Her breathing became forced, and hot flames raced through her.

An eternity later, when he lowered her hand, his eyes flashed their desire. Her mind fought its continuing conflict with her heart, reminding her of who he was and what he represented. Memories of Stephen and the pain he had caused arose, but those were soon chased away by the very conversations she and Sally had had over the last days. With Sally's admonitions fading in her mind, Michael's face reappeared.

Fear and desire split her in two. The need to love and be loved clashed with her refusal to be hurt. Logic and emotion fought a mighty battle for domination even as the burning touch of his lips on her hand remained strong.

"Don't be afraid, Alison. I will never hurt you," Michael promised. His words came from his heart, and he knew he would never break his promise.

With those words, Alison's heart swelled. The dam behind which she had hidden her emotions for so many years burst, and like a flood-maddened river, they rushed outward with all their power.

An instant later they were in each other's arms, their mouths joined, their arms tightly about each other, and their hearts beating almost in unison.

When the passionate kiss that spoke so much ended, Michael, with his arm around Alison's waist, started walking them toward Douglas's cottage.

"Please leave this message. Call Allan no matter what time. Urgent." Dr. Allan Worley, president and founder of Tri-Tech, listened as the operator repeated the message. When she was finished, he thanked her and hung up.

He shook his head slowly. He was bone tired. He'd been thinking of the thinly veiled threat he'd received from St. Clare's office. He had ignored work completely after talking to Alison, and had gone home to try to figure out what to do about the company he had founded six years before.

He had always been an idealist and Tri-Tech represented the manifestation of his dreams. For the first two years he had walked a narrow tightrope between solvency and bankruptcy. Then Alison Rand had joined the staff, and within a year, her genius had helped to make the huge profits necessary to prosper in the medical field.

In the last three years, Allan had gotten used to the idea of unlimited funds coming in to further his idealistic aims. Then Michael St. Clare had come to challenge and destroy him.

He admitted to himself that St. Clare, with the

media coverage that always followed him, frightened him. He'd caved in under Anne Harding's demands to have Alison debate St. Clare. He'd even gone as far as to almost order Alison to do it.

But after rethinking the aims of his company, and the good work they were doing, he could no longer sit by and let someone run roughshod over them. He and the rest of his staff had done nothing to be ashamed of, and he would not let Alison be used as a sacrificial lamb.

When she called, Allan planned to tell her exactly what had happened, and he would then release her from any obligations she might feel about appearing on the show.

Allan glanced at the phone. *Call me, Alison.*

Alison never saw the flashing red message light on her telephone because she had not gone to her room. She had gone with Michael, trapped within the grip of a passion she had not known she possessed.

Her mind reeled with confusion; her heart refused to slow its frantic beating. But her legs continued to hold her upright as Michael led her through the cottage and into the bedroom.

The only sounds she heard were those of her heart, her breathing, and the chorus of insects caroling in the woods behind the cottage.

Moonlight filtered in through two large windows, illuminating the room with a pale, iridescent sheen. The dark-paneled walls reflected nothing, but the highly polished brass headboard was alluring.

Michael turned her and kissed her deeply. Alison's mouth softened and her lips parted. His tongue met hers in a dance of passion, and Alison surrendered herself to him. Her arms wound around his back, her hands tracing over his firm muscles even as his strong hands caressed her skin through the silk dress.

Then Michael drew away; his eyes were soft and calm. "I need you, Alison," he whispered in a husky voice.

Once again, fear threatened to take control, but she bravely met his open gaze. Without speaking, she raised up on her toes and reached toward him.

When their lips met, the turmoil within her gave way. Her love and needs, so long repressed, burst forth to take command of her thoughts and movements. Although she knew that Michael St. Clare represented a danger to her career, she discovered that she could not hate him, and realized that the term "enemy" no longer held any meaning.

With a crystal clarity that was both a rarity and a revelation, Alison found that she could no longer hide behind the facade she created. She must heed what her heart had been crying for. She must take the chance and allow her emotions to be free so that she could live and love again.

With these revelations, Alison ended the kiss. Taking a deep, shuddering breath, she stared into Michael's eyes.

"I need you too, Michael. I . . . I didn't know how much until now." Her eyes were moist, but it didn't matter. She saw Michael start to speak, and her hand flew to his mouth.

"No. Don't say anything else. Don't make promises you can't keep. Just love me, Michael, please, love me."

Michael was aware of the change that was taking place within Alison. He could not say what he wanted to, or tell her the things that were within him, because he knew that the power of his emotions would frighten her with its depth. Instead, he drew her close again.

Tomorrow, he told himself.

Then he kissed her, and for the first time since he'd known Alison, he unleashed his need and desire for her. The subtle heat and softness of her lips overwhelmed his senses, and a moment later, he scooped her from the floor and drew her to him.

Alison was pulled upward, supported by his strong arms. His mouth was still upon her, and she felt as though she were floating a mile above the earth. His strength flowed through her, and when she reluctantly took her mouth from his, she buried her face into the joining of his neck and shoulder.

She was suddenly seduced by the scent of his masculinity, which clung so close to his skin. Her lips touched his neck, and she could feel the pulsing of his blood.

Carefully, gracefully, Michael lowered her to the bed while kissing her again and again. Outside, time raced by with the swiftness of the speeding world, but for Michael and Alison, time had come to a jarring halt.

Through a haze of maddening desires, Alison allowed herself to be undressed, unable to help Michael, although she wanted to. Whenever her hand tried to aid him, he would catch it, kiss it and then release it.

Without fully understanding how it happened, Alison was aware that she was naked, and that Michael, who had left the bed, had returned and was lying next to her. The heat emanating from his skin bathed her with a gentle warmth.

Michael gazed along the length of Alison's body,

his breath was bated, his mind tumbling with passion. The beauty of her slender form, accented by the graceful swell of her hips and the slightly raised outline of her stomach was a sight that would always live in his mind.

Her firm, peach-tipped breasts called to him, but he pulled his gaze from their beauty to look at Alison's face. Moonlight graced her skin, enhancing the subtle shadows to bring out all the mysterious beauty that was so much a part of her.

Her large blue eyes beckoned him. The double bow of her moist lips cried for his kisses. Without taking his eyes from hers, he lifted himself and kissed her.

Alison responded to his gaze, and then to his kiss with an abandon she had never before possessed. Her hands stroked his back and shoulders, her lips opened for him, and her tongue met his.

The kiss lasted for a long time, and as it lingered, her blood raced through her body. The kiss deepened, and his hand roamed along her shoulder sending sparks skittering across its surface.

Michael drew his mouth from hers and, moving slowly, trailed his lips over her closed eyelids, traced her high cheekbones and kissed the upturned corners of her mouth before lowering his lips to her neck and tasting its velvet surface.

His hands continued to caress her shoulders, but when his lips were at the base of her throat, feeling the vibrating of her heartbeat just below the surface of her skin, his hands went to her breasts and caressed them tenderly.

Soon his mouth wandered the same trail as his hands, and his lips blazed across her breast until they reached the first tender tip. He drew it into his mouth, tasting her nipple as if it were the rarest of delicacies.

Then he abandoned it, only to travel across the silken expanse of her chest to reach and lavish her other breast with equal attention.

Alison's body was alive with passion. Every movement that Michael made reverberated within her. Fire scorched her skin even as her blood turned to rushing lava. His lips were demanding and giving at the same time; his hands were gentle yet firm in their caresses.

His physical loving was an assault to her senses that she never wanted to end. But when he moved, and lifted himself from her, her eyes snapped open to stare at him.

"You are so beautiful," he said in a thick, emotion-laden voice. "So exquisitely beautiful."

Alison shuddered under the dual impact of his words and gaze. Then she too lifted herself and reached out to him. Their lips met, but this time it was Alison who kissed him so passionately. Her hands wandered along his back, caressing every inch of skin they could reach. Her breasts were crushed against his chest; her breath was almost cut off by the tightness of his hold, but she did not care. Then she pulled her lips from his and released her hands from his back. Slowly, she lifted them to cup his face.

She enjoyed the barely perceptible raspiness of his shaven face on her palms. Then her hands slid to the back of his head, and her fingers wound into his hair. Slowly, she began to lie back and drew Michael with her.

In that instant, their minds came together, even as their bodies did. A moment later, Michael was poised above her, his lips crushing down on hers, and his body covering hers completely.

The first fiery touch of him was like an ember burning on her skin. But without effort, she relaxed and accepted him. Then he was within her, filling her with himself as his arms pulled her tighter and his lips found the softness of her neck.

As they became one, Alison cried out and then buried her face on his shoulder. Lost within the beauty of what they had become, she was carried along by her passion and love.

The strength of his body flowed into hers. She moved with him, holding him tightly to her as the world disappeared, and reality became a place where only she and Michael lived and loved.

The rhythm of their bodies was but a reflection of their minds, and Alison continued to cast aside the barriers that were so much a part of her life. Without warning, her body tensed in a way that was so different, so new and so wonderful. She gave herself over to Michael, following him until they reached the very highest pinnacle of their lovemaking.

Alison tensed around him as Michael held her tightly. His mouth sought hers, and he kissed her deeply, even as their bodies shuddered together in the release of the love they had given one another.

When it was over, Michael could not let her go. He held her to him, lavishing her with kiss after kiss, until their breathing slowed and the wild beating of their hearts became more controlled.

But Michael still did not release her, rather, he pulled her with him as he turned onto his side. Alison did not protest; her body felt as though it had turned to rubber, and she needed the security of his arms around her.

She settled herself against him; one arm was bent, her palm against his chest. The other arm was wrapped around his torso, caressing the length of his back. She burrowed her face into his chest, and, unable to keep her eyes open in the aftermath of their explosive, all-consuming lovemaking, Alison fell asleep without realizing she had.

Michael inhaled the fragrance of her hair as his hand made slow circles in the small of her back. Now that they had indeed become lovers, he thought, it was time to tell her how he felt. "Alison," he whispered, kissing her head.

He waited for several seconds, but she did not answer. Then he heard the steady rhythm of her breathing and smiled to himself. She had fallen asleep.

Alison opened her eyes and looked at the unfamiliar surroundings. *It wasn't a dream,* she told herself. And then tension flooded her body.

She fought against it, and a moment later her muscles started to relax. She thought about last night and what had happened. She'd let herself go in a way she had never done before. Alison had given her love to Michael and had received no reassurances that he felt the same about her.

Even as she remembered their lovemaking, she experienced a pleasant flush that covered her body and took away the thoughts that were spoiling her memory.

She had not realized she'd fallen asleep, but sometime before dawn, she had woken within Michael's arms and seen him gazing at her. Wordlessly, they had come together again. This time their lovemaking was slower, but no less intense.

Afterward, they had lain in each others' arms, and when Alison had spoken to Michael, she found that this time it was he who had fallen asleep. She hadn't disturbed him; she'd gazed at him, drinking in his masculinity until her eyes closed again.

Can I face him now? she asked herself as she sat up, drawing the sheet with her. Looking around, she saw that her clothing was no longer on the floor, but draped across a chair.

What possessed me last night? Even as she asked herself the question, she discovered she knew the answer. She was in love with Michael; she had been since she'd first seen him. But she had held back, fighting against emotions that were so alien to her.

It had been Sally and Douglas who had proven to be the catalyst, making her see what she was denying herself. It was all Sally's doing with her nonadvice and good sense.

I took the risk, she told her absent friend.

Alison left the bed, picked her clothes off the chair as she passed it and went into the bathroom. After washing up and dressing, she emerged from the bathroom and tried to think what to do next. She had been unable to dispel her nervousness about seeing Michael this morning—after the intensity of their passion—and wondered what she would say to him.

Just as she took her first step toward the door it opened, and Michael, looking taller than ever, smiled at her. "Good morning."

"Good morning," Alison replied, aware of how his voice affected her and dispelled her nervousness. Without trying, she had relaxed.

Michael enfolded her within his arms. He kissed her gently. "Maybe short hair does have its advantages. You look wonderful this morning."

"I . . . thank you," she said, puzzled by his off-handed compliment. "You don't like my hair?" she asked.

"I love your hair."

Alison raised her eyebrows. "But you prefer women with long hair."

Michael heard the hint of challenge in her voice. "Until I met you I liked long hair," he said truthfully.

"Oh."

"Coffee?" he inquired.

Alison smiled fully. "I'd love some." Michael turned, and she followed him from the bedroom. She breathed a sigh of relief at how easy seeing him and speaking to him had been.

Michael took her to the back porch of Douglas's cottage, which faced the woods and was not visible from the rest of the resort complex. They sat at the table, and Alison drank the strong, but delicious coffee.

After several sips, she started to speak at the same time as Michael. They laughed and tried again with exactly the same results.

"You first," Alison said.

Michael shook his head. "Beauty before age."

"That's backward."

"I'm like that sometimes," he told her. "Please," he added. He wanted to tell her how he felt about her, about the love he knew was only for her, but he did not want any interruptions and was content to wait for her to finish speaking.

"All right. I . . ." she began, but paused for a moment to reorganize her thoughts. She held his gaze for another long moment. "I want to know about us. A few days ago we were opponents, fighting against each other's views. Last night we . . . we became lovers." She stopped then, knowing that in spite of her self-control she was blushing. "Where does that leave us?"

"In love?" Michael asked, his face devoid of amusement.

Alison heard his words, and her heart soared, but she could not give in to its song until she was certain. "I've been asked to debate you on television. How can I do that now?"

"You can't. Neither can I."

Alison breathed deeply. "Michael, I—"

Michael cut her off. He shook his head even as he reached across the table and grasped her hand. "I don't want to fight you. I don't want to do anything but love you. If you'll let me," he said.

"Michael . . ." But Michael stopped her again.

"Let me speak. It's not very often that two people can recognize how they feel about each other. It's less often that they act on their feelings. We acted last night. Now we have to make sure that we continue to do just that. I don't want to lose you, Alison."

Alison's throat tightened and a flood-tide of emotion swept over her. Her eyes misted; she blinked them clear. Then she squeezed his hand tighter. "Neither do I."

"Good!" he declared with a smile that made her heart skip a beat. "Then it's settled. No debates."

Alison nodded in agreement. "I'm surprised."

"About what?"

"That you'd stop fighting against the computer games."

Michael's brows knit together. Then he shook his

head. "I'm not stopping. I'm just not going to do battle with you."

Alison held back the sudden dashing of her spirits. She tried to digest his words, but could not. "Why, Michael?

"Because someone has to make the people understand the harm of those games."

Alison gazed at him while she slowly gained an understanding of the man who was a crusader. She remembered his story from yesterday, and remembered too the zeal that had permeated his words. She had known then that when he made up his mind, he would do everything in his power to win. But she had also sensed that behind it all had been the fact that he did what he believed in, and he believed that the games were hurting the kids who played them.

"Then it all comes back to us. What about us?" she asked again.

"We have to separate our personal and professional lives."

"Can we? Michael, you've already told me that your work is your life. Do you expect mine to be any less?"

Michael sighed. "No. I think we'll have to work it out. And, it won't be easy at all."

"No, it won't."

"But you'll try?" he asked, his eyes locking with hers.

"I'll try if you will."

"That's all we can do."

Alison, in a mood somewhere between elation and terror, returned to her hotel room, undressed, showered and then dressed again in a pair of jeans and a tee shirt.

Just as she was about to leave, she saw the red blinking message light on her phone. Picking the receiver up, she asked the operator for the message. A moment later she was dialing Allan's number, knowing that she must tell him that she wouldn't do the show.

"Hello," Allan answered on the third ring.

"I thought I'd try you at home first, seeing it's Saturday." Then she paused, trying to think of the right way to tell him. "About the show—"

"Wait. Alison, before you say anything, there's something you have to know." Without waiting for her reply, Allan told Alison about the coercion St. Clare's assistant had used. When he finished, he told her that he felt she shouldn't debate him, that Tri-Tech would weather this storm and that they would survive and continue doing the work they did best.

But Alison wasn't listening to him any longer. She was hearing Michael's persuasive coaxing of this morning, and feeling the way they had blended together so perfectly last night.

Her heart twisted as Alan continued speaking, and she had to close her eyes tightly. Her hands started to shake, and her throat constricted with pain. Tears streamed down her face, but her voice, when she spoke, remained firm. "Call the television station. Tell them I'll do the show."

"Alison, have you heard what I said?" Allan asked.

"Every last word," she told him. Then she hung up the phone and left the hotel room, gathering about her all the emotions that had been unleashed the night before. Until Michael had freed them, she had kept them hidden for years, she let her anger, pain and heartache combine to give her strength.

Only then, when her thoughts and emotions were centered on Michael St. Clare and what he had done to her, did she walk toward the dining room.

Chapter Seven

Alison stepped into the dining room and paused. Glancing around, she looked from table to table until she spotted Michael sitting across the room at a table for two.

With the full mass of her rage powering her steps, she walked directly toward him. He was gazing out the window; his face was relaxed, and she realized that he was far too handsome for her own good.

Then she was standing next to him. She waited until Michael sensed her presence and turned. When his eyes met hers, they seemed to light up, and again, Alison let her rage suffocate her passion.

As a smile stole on his lips, Alison's breath hissed sharply out. "Why, Michael?" Michael's brows knitted together, and Alison's heart skipped a beat.

"Why what?"

"You unfeeling bastard," she spat.

Before he could react, Alison bent over the table, picked up the water pitcher and dumped its contents over his head. Behind her she heard startled gasps from the other guests in the room.

Michael, reacting instinctively to the cold water, pushed his chair back and started to rise, but Alison's hand went to his shoulder and pressed him back into the seat.

Alison didn't know where she had gotten her surge of strength, but her hand was on his shoulder, and she refused to let him stand. "Don't move!" When she felt him stop fighting, she withdrew her hand.

"You unmitigated, lying, deceiving coward! Are you so afraid that I can show you up, can prove that you're wrong, that you had to play with my emotions in order to win?"

"Alison," he said, ignoring the water dripping down his face as he realized that Anne had not gotten through to Allan Worley in time. "I can explain."

"No, you can't! You used me! You came here to seduce me and to take away my will to fight you!"

Unable to stop it, anger built inside Michael; but before he could explain, Alison went on. "What was your game plan? To make me fall in love with you so that when I had to debate you, I wouldn't be able to?"

"That's not true," Michael said in a falsely calm voice.

"The hell it's not. If it isn't, then why did you blackmail my boss! But you made a mistake, Mr. Consumer Advocate. You lied to me. And damn it all . . . I'll see you on television!"

Alison spun on her heels and stormed out of the dining room, ignoring the startled and shocked stares of the witnesses.

* * *

"I'm really sorry," Anne Harding said.

"It's all right," Michael told her. Then he hung up the phone. A moment later he was on the back porch, looking at the tall pines. Whenever he embarked on a consumer campaign, he always planned everything down to the last detail. But over the past few days, his thoughts had been centered on Alison and not on work.

His biggest mistake, he realized, was in not telling Alison what had happened as soon as he'd known. Shaking his head, he tried to envision a way of making Alison listen to reason.

When he'd returned to the cottage, after Alison's water-accented tirade, he'd changed into dry clothes and called Anne at home. Although he already knew the answer, he'd asked her if she'd reached Dr. Worley. Anne had told him she'd been trying since they'd spoken, but Worley had not been in the office yesterday.

No matter what I tell her now, she won't believe me, he told himself, and knew that it was the truth. Yet he refused to accept that. As had been his habit, when there was something he wanted, he went after it with all his ability. His quest for Alison Rand would be no different, he would win her back.

An hour later, Michael was still sitting on the porch. He had thought it best to let Alison cool down before he talked to her and explained what had happened. He was sure that once she heard his explanation—heard the truth—things would be all right. Yet after the endlessly long hour, he could wait no longer.

Just as Michael left the chair, he heard the front door of the cottage open and Douglas call his name.

ENTER THE

Silhouette
Diamond
Sweepstakes

WIN The Silhouette Diamond Collection

Treasure the romance of diamonds.
Imagine yourself the proud owner of
$50,000 worth of exquisite diamond jewelry.

GLAMOROUS
DIAMOND
PENDANT

PRECIOUS
DIAMOND
EARRINGS

EXOTIC
DIAMOND
RING

CAPTIVATING
DIAMOND
BRACELET

Silhouette
Diamond
Sweepstakes

Rules and Regulations plus
entry form at back of this book.

Going inside, Michael found Douglas leaning against the fireplace, while Sally stood in the center of the room, glaring at him.

"Nice move," Douglas said with a shake of his head.

"It was a mistake."

"You bet it was," Sally retorted. "I warned you about her. I told you not to hurt her."

Michael met Sally's glare with unfeigned honesty. "I hadn't meant to hurt her, Sally. It was a mistake, and I'll accept the blame."

"Which does Alison not one damned bit of good."

Michael stiffened at her words. The rage that he had been fighting since Alison had faced him in the dining room exploded.

"And it does me no good either! Do you think I like what happened? Do you think I planned it this way? For the first time in my life I've found a woman I can love without reservation, whom I'm happy being with, and who can make me feel that there is more to life than racing around from city to city."

"So in order to insure her devotion to you, you lied to her. That's a perfect way to start a relationship," Sally stated sarcastically.

"There was a mix-up at the office. Things were done without my knowledge. And damn it, Sally, I don't lie!"

Sally stared at him, unmoved by his declaration. "That doesn't excuse it from happening."

"No, it doesn't. Now, if you're through with me, I'm going to talk some sense into Alison."

"I don't think so," Sally said.

"I do."

"Then you'd better see how fast that fancy car of

yours will go, Michael, my friend, because she drove out of here a half-hour ago," Douglas informed him in a level voice.

"What?" he asked, looking from Sally to Douglas.

"She's gone, Michael," Douglas said. "We got back almost an hour ago. As soon as we drove in, Alison asked Sally for her car."

"And you let her?"

"Easy, friend," Douglas cautioned.

Sally cut in quickly. "At first she wouldn't tell me what happened," Sally said, "but I got the story from her. Then I helped her put her suitcases in the car."

"I'm going after her," Michael stated.

"Why, Michael, to torture her, to make her feel even more like a fool? Leave her alone. She's been hurt enough."

"I can't leave her alone."

"Why?"

Michael stared into Sally's eyes. "Because I love her."

Sally shook her head in exasperation. "You have a unique way of showing it."

"It was a mistake!" Michael growled, defending himself once again and angry with himself for having to do so.

Sally looked at Douglas and saw him nod imperceptibly. It was a signal that she was certain meant that Michael was telling the truth. She looked at Michael again. "Why didn't you tell her that?"

"I thought I had. We talked about it this morning. I thought she understood."

"All she understands is that you've made her into a fool."

"I'm going after her." Without waiting, Michael walked out of the cottage and went to his car. His suitcase was unpacked in his room, but he didn't think about that. All he thought of was Alison.

Alison stretched and blinked her eyes. She was exhausted, but she was afraid to stop. From the moment she'd left Tall Pass, she'd been haunted by the combination of love and desire that Michael had awakened within her. At the same time, she was assaulted by the incredible pain and hurt of what he had done to her.

She had driven straight from the dude ranch to Tri-Tech and had gone to her office, where she did her best to lose herself in her work.

But no matter how much she tried, with every idea she used, and every line she typed into the computer, she found herself fighting Michael's image and memory.

"Miss Rand," came the security guard's voice.

Alison turned to find Joseph standing in the doorway. "Yes?"

"It's midnight."

"I . . . all right," Alison replied. She turned back to the computer keyboard, typed in a new command, and a moment later the screen went blank. Standing, she stretched out the kinks in her back as she left her office.

The only time Tri-Tech was completely shut down was from Saturday at midnight until Sunday at noon for the labs and the computer offices to be cleaned, and for the computer systems to be inspected for any maintenance problems. That, and one other reason.

Because Tri-Tech had government contracts in aerospace technology, the government insisted on weekly checks to make sure that no electronic spying devices had been secreted into the offices. Alison had thought it to be a silly precaution, until she had read about another company in the valley that had been the victim of spies, and had lost a valuable secret to another country.

Alison walked through the empty corridor, and when Joseph let her out, she went directly to the car. *I don't want to go home,* she said to herself. But she knew she had no place else to go.

Michael sat in the driver's seat of the prototype car, parked directly across from Alison's apartment. He had been there for three hours, waiting for her to come home.

When he'd returned to San Francisco, he'd gone to his office and spent the afternoon calling her. All he'd gotten was her answering machine. Then he'd called Tri-Tech, but they were closed and no one answered.

After waiting until dark, and trying Alison's number every fifteen minutes, he'd decided to drive to Silicon Valley, and to her apartment house.

While he'd waited, he'd done a lot of thinking, but had come to no conclusions. As he let his mind drift again, he saw the wash of headlights turn onto the street.

Watching, as he had done with every car that passed, he waited to see where this one would go. The headlights approached him slowly, but before they reached him, the car turned into the parking lot of Alison's building.

The car pulled into an empty space and the driver got out. Whoever it was was deep in the shadows, but a moment later, as the figure walked under an overhead light, Michael, recognized Alison's blond capped head.

Without hesitating, he left the car and strode

toward her. When her hand was on the doorknob, Michael reached her side. "Alison," he whispered.

Alison was bone tired and prayed that when she was inside, sleep would claim her quickly. As she approached the entrance of the building, her key already in her hand, she looked neither left or right. When she put the key into the lock, she sensed someone come up to her. Then she heard his voice.

Whirling, she stared into Michael's eyes. "Go away!"

"No," he said simply. "Not until we get things straightened out."

"You've already done that. Please leave me alone." But even as she said it, she could feel turmoil building within her.

"Alison, I can't let this happen." Michael gazed at her, wanting to take her in his arms, kiss her and make her see how he felt.

Seeing the intensity in his eyes, Alison took a step away from him. She shook her head slowly, her arms held stiffly before her, warding him off. "Last night you promised you wouldn't hurt me. Today you did just that. Please, Michael, please leave me alone."

"You don't mean that. You don't want me to go!"

Alison's breath caught. She stared at him, unable to believe the audacity of his words. "Is that the effect you think you have on me? Don't flatter yourself!" she said in an icy voice.

Unreasonable anger welled within him. He had spent three hours sitting in a car, waiting for her, and all she could say to him was that she wanted him to go away. The anger grew, and as it did, he threw caution to the fates.

"I don't chase women around in order to hurt them."

"I'm sure you don't! What you do is try to win what you want in any way you can!"

"This is ridiculous." Michael almost shouted the words at her. "A mistake was made. That's all it was. Damn it Alison, can't you admit that you love me?"

Alison's heart stopped for a fraction of a second as his words struck her. She shook her head, trying to comprehend what was happening. Then she drew, from deep within her well of resolve, the calm that was necessary to face him.

"Is that what you want to hear? Do you want accolades to your masculinity? Do you want your victim . . . want me . . . to fall down at your feet and gaze up at you with wide, idolizing eyes?" Her questions were calm, cold and harsh, and they struck him in just the way she intended.

Michael's eyes narrowed and his lips tightened into a narrow band as he stared at her. Rage mixed with desire fueled his retort. "I was wrong about you," he stated. "I thought you were different, but you're not. You're just like all the other people who live by the almighty computer. I did make a mistake, but not the one I thought I did. I should have realized that like a computer, your heart is as cold as silicon."

Alison's face drained of blood. She could hear a buzzing in her head and thought that she would go mad. A hundred things came to mind, but she refused to allow another word to pass her lips. Moving slowly, she turned her back to him, opened the door and stepped inside. When the door was secured, she went up to her apartment, and once inside, she double-locked the door.

Only then did the tears she had refused to shed pour from her eyes. "Yes, damn you, I love you!" she whispered.

Alison spent all day Sunday deep in thought. She replayed, over and over, everything that had happened from the moment she had met Michael St. Clare until she learned the true nature of the man, and what he would do to make sure he came out on top.

She berated herself for falling into the neatly developed trap Michael had set for her, and reviled herself for being gullible enough to be caught unprepared. As she had done years before, she began to erect the walls that would renew her defenses against the world, and especially against Michael St. Clare.

Her outrage at what he had done remained a strong force. Although she tried to ease her heartache and fuel the fires of her resolve, she found a new feeling being born.

She remembered the way her mind and heart had soared when she'd released her pent-up emotions. She remembered how wonderful and free she'd felt. *Do I want to lose that too?* she asked herself.

If Michael had done nothing else, he had shown her that there was more to life than work. But even though she knew this, the pain of his deception continued to ache.

Her shame made her want to cringe. But she refused to succumb; instead, she channeled her thoughts and strove to rebuild her strength. Michael had challenged and insulted her. He had used her to gain an advantage, and she had allowed it to happen. Now, she must find a way to turn the tables on him.

She would not hide behind a wall of solitude. She would not seek solace in work; she would find a way to make herself whole again—to become a person, not just a shell.

Late on Sunday night, Sally called. Alison assured her that she was all right, and cut off Sally's apology for butting into her life.

"You were right. I have been living my life in a shell. But I'm a survivor, Sally."

She had ended the conversation in an optimistic mood, promising Sally that they would get together as soon as Sally returned home. Then she went to bed, but as she tried to fall asleep she could not cast aside the ghost of Michael, or her feelings of betrayed love.

On Monday morning, when she walked into Tri-Tech, she went directly to Allan Worley's office.

"You're still on vacation."

"I have work to do if I'm going to be on that show."

"You don't have to be. Alison, I don't want to see you chewed up and spit out by St. Clare."

You're looking at the end result, she wanted to say. "He won't," she said instead.

"Don't be naive," Allan cautioned.

"Not anymore. Allan, can I disrupt the schedule for a few days?" she asked.

Allan gazed at her for a moment, wondering what she had in mind. "For a good enough reason."

"I need ammunition. I need help to gather information."

"That we can do."

"Good. I'll need three people and video equipment."

"Done."

"I'm going to beat him, Allan. I'm going to teach

that egotistical, so-called do-gooder a lesson," Alison declared.

"What happened, Alison?" Allan asked in a calm voice.

"Without going into detail, he made me mad!"

Allan stared at her for several seconds and saw within the depths of her eyes just how true her words were. Slowly, very slowly, he nodded his head.

Anne Harding stood at the door to Michael's office. For the first time in all the years she'd worked for him, she hesitated before going inside.

She didn't know what was happening to him, but she was aware of the startling change in almost everything he did and said. He was brusque with her and everyone else on the staff, and surly with whomever he spoke to on the phone.

Although he had not said anything further to Anne about the Tri-Tech incident, she believed that it was part of the reason behind his mood. That, and Alison Rand.

She knocked on the door, opened it slowly and went inside. "Michael."

Michael turned from the window to look at Anne. He didn't speak; he just raised his eyebrows.

"Alison Rand will be debating you on the 'Afternoon Show' for the entire week. On the Sunday after the shows, you're scheduled to speak at the computer conference. You will be the main speaker, and will be speaking on the danger of computer games on youth. After you speak, Ms. Rand will reply to your comments."

"Will there be an armed guard?" he asked sarcastically.

"To protect them?" she asked. Then she shook her head. "Michael, can we talk seriously?"

Michael heard the undercurrent in her voice and took a deep breath. "Go ahead."

"What happened between you and Alison Rand?"

Michael laughed dryly. Then he shook his head. "It doesn't matter."

"It does. You've lost that spark of energy that pushes us all to do our best. You've been sitting here all week long looking at facts and figures, compiling statistics, but saying nothing. Why?"

"Have I?" he asked, feeling the intensity of her words.

"You know you have. Michael, you can't fight the computer industry with facts and figures. They have them all. They can manipulate them better than we can. You need yourself. You need that special drive which only you can produce."

Michael nodded but said nothing. Anne sighed and walked out of the office, closing the door gently behind her. She could only hope that whatever was disrupting his usual dynamic personality would leave him by Monday at one o'clock.

In the quiet office, Michael sat back in the chair and thought about what Anne had said, and found it impossible to deny the truth of her words. That night in front of Alison's apartment building had affected him deeply.

He had said things he shouldn't have, and she had reacted strongly. Instead of telling her that he loved her, he had asked if she loved him. Then his anger had gained the upper hand, and he'd lashed out thoughtlessly, defensively and accusatively.

After she had disappeared, he had walked for hours, trying to figure out a way to repair the damage.

But dawn had found him no closer to a solution than he'd been shortly after midnight.

For the rest of the week, he'd closeted himself in his office, studying the statistics his research team had uncovered. He read a hundred reports by teachers whose students wasted their minds in video parlors, and who did not put half of that effort into schoolwork. But the reports had blurred into each other.

Above it all, Alison's large blue eyes and short blond hair kept floating in the air before him. Her gaze was reproachful, her eyes challenging.

Closing his eyes, he thought about that one wonderful night when he and Alison had found the right path to walk and had become one.

He remembered the swelling of his love, the freeing of his emotions and the needs that had held him a captive to her charms. He had loved her from the first, and he could not let his love die because of a misunderstanding.

"No more!" he shouted. Standing, he began to pace the room. When he stopped, he went to his desk and pressed the intercom.

"Yes?" Anne asked.

"Get me Alison Rand."

He snapped the intercom off and waited.

Five minutes later Anne's voice harshly, interrupted the silence. "She's working at home and refuses to speak with you."

Without replying, Michael went to the door. As he stepped into the outer office, the receptionist's head snapped around. Anne Harding glanced up from her desk and watched Michael stride across the room and step into the waiting elevator. A moment later the door closed.

Anne smiled; once again she saw that magical, powerful aura surrounding Michael.

Alison gave her home computer the command to print out the latest file she had received, and when that was finished, she shut the unit down.

"That's the last of it," she told Sally as she stood.

"Good. Now can we go look for my wedding dress?"

"Sure."

Alison grabbed her purse as Sally rose. But before they reached the door, there was a knock.

"Expecting company?" Sally asked.

"No," she said as she went to the door and opened it. Her breath caught while her eyes drank in Michael's face.

"I'm glad they don't keep the front door locked during the day. May I come in?"

"No, we're just going out." Although it took all her strength, she kept her voice steady.

Michael's gaze flicked from Alison's face to Sally's. "Hi," he said to her. "Alison, I have to speak to you, now."

"You'll have to wait until Monday, at one," she told him, a trace of irritation marring the smooth put-down.

"It can't wait," Michael stated, refusing to move out of the doorway.

"I don't want to have a scene."

"Then invite me in."

Alison looked helplessly at Sally, who was suddenly looking somewhere else. Outside, she saw that several of her neighbors, who were sitting around the swimming pool in the building's courtyard, were looking up at them. Silently, she stepped back and allowed Michael to enter.

Careful, she warned herself, knowing that any misstep might be fatal.

"Thank you," Michael said when he closed the door behind him. Then he glanced at Sally. "Could we be alone for a moment?"

Sally started forward. "I'll be at the—"

"No, you won't! You'll be right here," Alison ordered. Then she glared at Michael. "How dare you come into my house and order my friend out."

"I wanted this to be private."

"Sally knows everything."

Michael shook his head slowly. "I'm not in love with Sally."

"No, you're only in love with yourself."

Michael drew his shoulders back. His eyes narrowed for a split-second. "I don't deserve that."

"No, you deserve much more."

"Alison, I came here to apologize, I came to tell you that I'm sorry for what happened, and that it should never have gone as far as it did." The moment the words were out, Michael knew that she'd taken them the wrong way.

Her face blanched, and her entire body stiffened. She stared at him with wide, disbelieving eyes, and then shook her head. "You're damned right it should never have happened. But I trusted you. I believed in you. Stupid, wasn't I?"

"Stop it!" Michael roared. His shout echoed wildly in the room. "Stop twisting everything I say to suit your own needs. Who do you think you are? Your indignant righteousness is making me sick. This is the second time I've come to you to apologize and explain what happened. But do you let me? No! All you can do is stand there wrapped in self-pride, and tell me what a miserable bastard I am. Well, lady, let me tell you something. Open your eyes, open your ears, and start to see and hear what's around you. Maybe then you'll understand what it means to be in love!"

"Me?" Alison screamed back at him. She took a step closer to him, and glared into his face. "You're telling me about self-pride? You're telling me to look around? Why don't you look in a mirror and see what self-pride is! You wear your pride like a mantle. And don't lecture me about love, not until you learn the meaning of the word." Alison's anger wiped away any hesitation and fear that she had of being too close to Michael. As the last word faded away, they were barely an inch apart.

Suddenly she could feel the closeness of their bodies, but knew she must not retreat. "And don't ever raise your voice to me, especially in my home!"

"Alison, I love you."

Alison refused to listen. She deflected his declaration as if she wore armor. She shook her head quickly. "You don't love me, you love the conquest. You seduced me, and you thought you conquered me. You didn't, Michael St. Clare, you just put yourself into a harder fight. Get out!"

"No." The word was so low that she thought she misunderstood him. But as she glared at him she realized he had said it. "Not until you let me explain."

Alison's breath exploded from her chest. "Then I'll leave." Turning, she looked at Sally, who was now staring at them wide-eyed. "Are we going to find that dress or not?"

Sally sighed as she looked from Michael to Alison. Then she nodded her head.

"Good," Alison declared. A moment later she opened her door. "I would advise you to be gone when I get back."

Once they were on the sidewalk outside the building, Alison stopped to take a deep breath. She looked at Sally and saw that her friend was once again avoiding her gaze. Anger and frustration constricted her chest, and she felt as though she had just run a hundred miles.

But with the frustrations came the knowledge that she had faced him and had not fallen apart. She had stood up to him. Relief, mixing with a strange and illusive sadness, washed over her.

"Can you believe that? Can you believe his utter gall?" she asked. Then she answered her own question as her anger again ebbed and flowed. "No! What does he want? Does he think he can scare me any more than he already has?"

Alison turned to look up at the second floor of her building. Then she remembered what he had said. *I love you.* But she would not let herself think about that. Not now—not ever. "I suppose you have something to say to me?" Alison challenged Sally.

When Sally's eyes reached Alison's, she could not hold her straight face any longer. "Ali—" but her words were cut off by a bubbling laugh that grew stronger each time she tried to stop.

Finally, when she was able to control herself, she shook her head. "Bravo, Alison! You were magnificent."

Alison, whose anger had again welled when Sally started laughing at her, held back her first acrid retort.

"Really," Sally said, "you really gave it to him. Wow, I thought he was going to explode."

"There's only one problem," Alison admitted.

"Only one?"

"For right now. If I threw him out of my apartment, why are we out here and Michael's still inside?"

Another gale of laughter overcame Sally. When she stopped and took several gulping breaths, she shrugged her shoulders. "What are you going to do now?"

Alison looked at her. "I thought you were the one who had all the answers?"

"You went way over my head in there." Then Sally's face settled into serious lines. "Alison, he does love you."

Alison closed her eyes. "But he loves his work more, and he's going to try and destroy what I represent."

"Then show him he's wrong."

"I'm going to do more than show him," she stated. "Sally, why does love hurt so much?"

"Because when it doesn't, it's wonderful?"

"Sally . . ."

"Yes?"

"I can't look at wedding dresses today."

Sally smiled. "I understand. Listen, the wedding isn't for another month, we have plenty of time."

"Thank you," she whispered. "Now, let's get out of here until Michael leaves."

Sally nodded her head and, seeing Alison's warning look, choked back her laughter.

Chapter Eight

$\mathcal{I}$ don't know," Alison said as she looked at herself in the dressing room's large mirror and studied the fit of the stylish dress.

"Alison, what do I do for a living?" Sally asked.

"Write magazine articles."

"Specifically?"

"Women's magazine articles," Alison responded.

"Exactly. And one thing I know is that you have to make the right impression. There will be tens of thousands of people watching you—"

"Thanks—"

"—today. You have to have a certain look."

"This is a debate, not a fashion show."

"Alison, you must trust me. Most people's idea of computers, and the people who work with them, is that they're cold. That's the operative word, cold. Machines are cold; therefore, people who work with them are cold too. If you wear that gray business suit, you're only exacerbating the situation."

"Really, I thought I was being comfortable," Alison rejoined, knowing that she and Sally were beating a dead horse. But arguing with Sally eased her nerves to a degree.

"Comfortable, maybe, appealing, no. You have to show a human side. You have to be the opposite of a machine. This dress will help."

Alison again looked at her image. The dress was far from casual; yet it did not look overly elegant. The light blue cotton was a nice contrast to her tanned arms and face, and although it had a trifle more decolletage than she liked, she knew that it also showed she was a real flesh and blood woman, not an animated machine.

Her hairstyle had been changed also by the studio hairdresser, again under Sally's guidance. Instead of her blond hair being brushed away from her face, the stylist had swept it to the side, leaving a fine veil of whispy bangs on her forehead.

"We need you in the Green Room, Ms. Rand," came the voice of the assistant producer.

Alison nodded silently and turned toward the door. "Sally."

"Yes?"

"I couldn't be a machine. The way I'm shaking, I would have fallen apart by now."

Sally said nothing; instead, she took Alison's hand in hers and started walking. "Remember," she finally said at the door, "when they introduce you, stand and look up into Michael's face. Make the camera see how petite you are, and how big an ogre he is."

"I'll try," Alison promised.

Once they were inside, the room was empty, but Alison had expected that. When she'd spoken to the producer of the show, she'd insisted that she and Michael be separated until the show began.

The man had agreed, evidently looking forward to the show that he would be airing. Two hours before, she had met with John Lawson, the host of the "Afternoon Show." She had been impressed with his relaxed style and intelligent questions. But she had gone tense when he'd referred to the newspaper article in yesterday's paper, which had proclaimed, in a large headline on the entertainment page, "the battle of the century."

The article had encapsulated Alison and Michael's appearance on the late-night talk show, and had lauded Alison's maneuver of walking off. The reporter had ventured to say that he thought this week's show would be a lively feud that would indeed be educational.

John Lawson had extracted a promise from Alison that she would not walk off his show. In return, he granted her the right to bring on a guest on the last day if she wanted to.

"Ms. Rand." Alison sat straighter when her name was called. "It's time. You're on first."

Alison looked at Sally.

"Go get him," Sally whispered.

"I'm scared to death," Alison admitted.

"Me too," Sally replied. "Go on."

Without looking back, Alison followed the assistant producer to the sound stage and stepped inside. Once again her senses were assaulted by the myriad of equipment, and the seeming lack of cohesion in the atmosphere.

A moment later everything was quiet. A man, complete with the requisite clipboard, was counting down seconds as he stared at a stopwatch.

"Three. Two. One. On the air," he said, flicking the watch and pointing to John Lawson. The assistant producer took her elbow and slowly led her to the edge of the stage while the host spoke.

Sooner than she wanted it to happen, John Lawson introduced her. Taking a deep breath, she went out onto the set, feeling a wave of heat from the multitude of lights strike her harshly.

All the spectator seats in the studio had been filled, and the audience was large enough to make a lot of noise with their applause. When Alison reached John Lawson, she shook his hand and smiled at the audience before sitting down.

"Miss Rand is not just any employee in Silicon Valley," John Lawson told the audience, "she is the designer of the single most popular video game in the country right now. *The Wizard of Fantasy.*"

Another round of applause greeted this statement and Alison's nerves peaked with the noise. "But more important than that," Lawson went on, "Alison Rand is the champion of the computer game industry, who has come here to do battle with a man whom everyone knows, and therefore needs no introduction. Michael St. Clare."

Alison's heart began to beat in time with the loud applause, louder, she realized than her welcome had been. She sat still while he walked onto the stage, and drew strength from her iron self-control.

After Michael shook Lawson's hand, he stepped toward Alison. Reacting quickly, Alison rose and offered him her hand. When he took it, she made believe her arm did not exist, and that the tingling warmth was but a figment of her imagination.

Then Michael was smiling at her. Her breath caught before she realized what was happening. Willing a firmer control over her reactions, and following Sally's advice, Alison tilted her head back much further than was necessary in order to look up at him.

Silence was the rule for the moment, but John Lawson quickly took control as he guided Michael to the seat on his left. When everyone was seated, Lawson started the conversation.

"The last time the two of you met, it was on another show. You seemed to have gotten into quite an argument, if I recall correctly."

Alison beat Michael by a half-second. "To be honest, and to set the record straight," Alison said, looking from Lawson to the audience and back again, "I had been invited on the show to talk about *The Wizard of Fantasy*. I had no idea that Mr. St. Clare had also been invited, and his appearance was as much of a surprise to me as was his attack."

"There was no attack on you, only, what you represent!" Michael snapped.

"Really? Then what would you call telling me that my game corrupted the youth of this country? Praise?" Alison sat back then, forcibly keeping the smile from her face. She was amazed at how quickly her nerves had settled; she was ready to challenge Michael. She also knew that she must gain the initiative and keep it for as long as possible.

"I said that it was computer games in general that were hurting the youth of the country."

"Subverting, I believe the word was." With that she saw John Lawson's smile. Then she saw Michael shrug.

"Miss Rand," Lawson said, stepping in as soon as he realized there would be no further response, "Mr. St. Clare had stated several times that computer games, both the home videos and the arcade games are undermining our educational systems. Would you respond to that, please."

"Not without an explanation of how Mr. St. Clare means that."

Michael smiled. "That is exactly what I'm talking about. Computers are taking away society's ability to reason. The games the kids are playing are the prime example. The instructions, detailing every last item, leave nothing to chance. Without those instructions, the person cannot function. This very problem is being carried over into their everyday lives. But," he said as he heard the low laughs he'd elicited from the audience, "to answer Ms. Rand . . . what I meant was that the youth, and I mean those children between the ages of eight and eighteen, are spending more time shooting down alien invaders, killing flying bugs and maneuvering pills that eat ghosts than they are studying."

"Surely, Mr. St. Clare, that's not the games' fault. The lack of stimulation in their classrooms must have some responsibility for the youth looking elsewhere. And what about the parents? Aren't they the people who buy the video games for their children. Aren't you attacking them also?"

Alison sat back, her smile not too big, her eyes just wide and innocent enough not to seem as though she were feigning her reactions while she waited for Michael's response. Yet, she was still unable to make the tingling from the contact of his hand on hers go away. *Damn you!* she cried silently.

"Very nice," Michael said. Then he looked at Lawson. "Did she answer the question, or ask one?"

Again the audience laughed. Alison stiffened. Anger rose sharply, and she tried to keep herself under control. "I thought I had. But I'll try again, since Mr. St. Clare so evidently doesn't want to hear an opposing viewpoint. Computer games are interesting, educational and exciting. The youth who play them are getting the stimulation they apparently can't get in a classroom.

"And," she continued before Michael could start talking again, "the games are far from subverting our youth. The only evidence I know of that supports Mr. St. Clare's position is only what he himself has said. He has not offered anything to substantiate his claims." Alison paused to look at the audience. "Other than, of course, his own conjecture. Isn't that correct?" she asked, turning back to face him.

"I'm sorry, but I'll have to interrupt. Ladies and gentlemen, we'll be back after these words from our sponsor." As soon as Lawson finished, he smiled. "Wonderful. Just keep it up for the next ten minutes," he told them both.

"Alison," Michael called in a low voice. Alison looked at him and waited. "I love your apartment."

"I should have called the police," she shot back. Her eyes shifted briefly to John Lawson's, and she saw an interesting glint in his eyes.

"Why didn't you?"

"Then you'd be in jail, and Mr. Lawson would have had to cancel this stimulating show."

"Fifteen seconds," called the man with the clock and clipboard.

"What's going on?" Lawson asked them both.

Alison sat back on the couch and ignored Michael and John Lawson. The show was on again.

"Welcome back to the "Afternoon Show." I'm John Lawson, and with me are Alison Rand and Michael St. Clare. And let me tell you folks something, especially our viewers at home. We've got a real battle on our hands. A fight that's going to last all week long. Now, Alison, you responded last, so I'll direct my next question to Michael St. Clare. Michael, you've never been known to attack anything in a frivolous manner. Ms. Rand seems to think you're directing your energies against the computer games with no valid reason. Is that so?"

"Hardly. The reason I've become so involved in this is because of the amount of letters my organization has received from teachers and parents who are at a loss about what to do. It started two and a half years ago, and the deeper I delved into the problem, the more convinced I became that computer games were becoming a danger."

"Just like rock and roll was in the fifties?" Alison shot, unable to help herself.

"You're drawing the wrong parallels," Michael told her. Then he continued in the high-handed manner with which he'd started. "In one early case, a boy of fifteen had to undergo intensive therapy to stop his obsession with video games."

Once again Alison's temper flew out of control. "And in one case," she said in a loud voice, "a teenage girl tried to commit suicide when a famous singer got married. There are always people with obsessive personalities!"

Michael shook his head slowly. Then he stood and looked at John Lawson. "Until you can keep Ms.

Rand under control, and allow me to answer my questions without interruptions, I will not be able to continue with this charade."

Alison, a sinking sensation twisting her stomach, watched Michael walk off the sound stage. Fighting her temper down, Alison looked at the audience and shrugged. "I didn't think I scared him that much. After all, he's so much bigger than I."

The audience clapped their approval of her words. John Lawson leaned forward in his chair. "Now I understand how Dan Marshal felt when you walked out on him. But, Ms. Rand, I will have to insist on Mr. St. Clare's demands."

"All right," Alison said. "Call him back." But even as she spoke, she saw a cardboard sign held up. *St. Clare out of studio.*

"Well, I guess we will give Mr. St. Clare the rest of the day to cool down. Perhaps we could use the time remaining to answer any questions from the studio audience? Yes?" he said as he pointed to a teenage girl.

Alison sighed. She knew that Michael had planned out this course of action. There could be no other explanation. But she pushed that from her mind and, while answering the girl's question, thrust aside the strange longing that had started when he'd walked away.

Alison sat in her darkened living room, staring at nothing in particular while she tried to relax enough to think about sleep.

The day had been a very long one, filled with tension, anxieties, and spurts of relief. When the television show had ended, Alison had returned to the dressing room and changed, while Sally, who had watched the whole thing in the Green Room, kept up a running commentary.

When they'd left the building, Alison was beginning to feel the let-down of the morning's excitement, and did not want to talk about Michael or the show. Sally, as thoughtful as always, had accepted her wishes.

When they'd returned to Alison's apartment, her phone had started to ring incessantly with friends and co-workers calling to congratulate her for showing up St. Clare.

Finally, after speaking with her boss, Alison disconnected her telephone. "I didn't beat him today," she'd said to Sally.

"I know," Sally had replied. "But you were doing so well that he had to do something to shake you and the audience up."

"He did do that," Alison had admitted.

"What about you?" Sally had asked. Her eyes had darkened with the question, and her face had turned very serious. "How did you feel when you were facing him?"

"Funny, I guess. I tried to pretend I didn't know him, that he was a stranger, but every time he spoke or looked at me, I felt betrayed."

"He says it was all a mistake. He claims he didn't know what had been said to Allan."

"I find that hard to believe," Alison had told Sally. She too had been thinking about that ever since Sally told her of Michael's explanation. "Michael St. Clare is his organization. After spending all of last week researching it, and him, I know that he controls every move that's made."

Before they could delve any deeper into the subject, there had been a knock on the door. Sally stood, signaling Alison to stay seated. From the couch, Alison had seen Sally open the door, give a squeal of delight, and then go into a tight embrace. A moment later, she had led Douglas into the living room.

That was the first time Alison remembered that Douglas was picking Sally up. They would be returning to the resort that night.

"Look at what I found outside," Sally had declared with a wide smile.

Alison had smiled in greeting to Sally's fiancé, and had felt a genuine happiness for her friend.

"Sorry to barge in, but I've been calling since three without any luck."

"You're not barging in, you're expected. Did you see the show?" Alison had asked.

"No," Douglas had replied with a smile. "I don't watch fights when I can't pick sides."

"Very diplomatic," Alison had replied.

"That's my man," Sally had stated proudly.

A wave of sadness had engulfed Alison, but she'd dismissed it with a bright smile. "How's everything at Tall Pass?"

"Fine, just lonely. Oh," Douglas had said, "I brought the afternoon paper." With that he'd handed it to Alison. "Look on the back page."

Alison had, and as she read the headline, her breath caught as she looked at the picture of herself watching Michael walk off the stage. "What does it say?" Sally had asked.

Alison had looked up at her friend. "Round one—a walk off draw. Score, one to one."

"Oh, boy," Sally had whispered.

Alison had cast the paper away from her. She hadn't wanted to read it. Then, Sally's smile had brightened.

"Can we take you out for dinner?"

"I'm not hungry," Alison had responded. "Besides, I won't be fit company, and you two have a four-hour drive ahead of you. So go!" she had ordered with a false cheeriness.

Sally had looked at her, concern on her face. "Alison, I can stay for the week. . . ."

"Thank you for today, Sally. I really needed you. But I think I can handle the rest of the week." Then she had looked at Douglas. "Get her out of here before I change my mind."

"Alison . . ." Douglas began, but she had cut him off.

"Please. I'm a big girl and I can handle this myself."

"Alison," Sally had chimed in with a calm voice, "just remember to wear the dresses in the order I set them out."

"I will," she had promised. Then she'd stood and gone to Sally, embraced her friend, and then embraced Douglas. "Thank you, both of you."

They had left, but not before Alison had seen the hesitation cross Sally's face again. But Douglas, seeing Alison's determination, had coaxed Sally to leave.

Once Alison was alone, she had spent the rest of the evening deep in thought, wondering what tomorrow would bring.

Alison yawned, and brought her mind back to the present. She was getting sleepy at last. Just as she started to stand, her eye caught the newspaper she had tossed so carelessly away. Knowing she was making a mistake, she reached for it and began to read the article under the back page headline.

Today's main event was not on prime-time television, but on midday programming. The "Afternoon Show" was the boxing ring, and the opponents were consumer advocate Michael St. Clare, and software author Alison Rand.

These two combatants have only appeared together once before, on Dan Marshall's late-night talk show, but that meeting will live on in the annals of television as the first round of what is shaping up to be a real battle of wills.

Michael St. Clare's latest campaign in consumer protection is directed against the computer industry, and computer games specifically. Usually, St. Clare is rarely opposed because of the negative publicity that his appearances generate for his opposition.

But in this instance, the computer industry has found a worthy proponent in Alison Rand, who, for all her diminutive size, is a real fighter. After walking off one television show where St. Clare was an unannounced guest who attacked her and her profession, she agreed to a series of debates to prove that St. Clare was operating under a misconception.

As of the end of the first round on the "Afternoon Show," this reporter was unable to determine if either of the views presented was valid. But one thing this reporter is sure of, the next four days will be an exciting time.

Watching Rand and St. Clare battle reminds one of nothing less than a good Spencer Tracy— Katharine Hepburn romantic movie. All I can say is

*that this reporter will most definitely keep tuned to the
fireworks for the rest of the week.*

Alison groaned when she read the last paragraph.
Hepburn and Tracy? she asked herself.

When Michael had left the studio, he'd claimed his
car and driven out of the city. He'd gone to a lovely
stretch of wooded land and spent the afternoon there,
deep in thought. When he'd returned home, well after
dark, he'd found Anne Harding waiting for him with a
newspaper in her hands.

After they'd entered the apartment, Anne had
handed him the paper, and had sat across from him in
his large living room.

A few moments later Michael finished the article
and folded the paper. When he looked at Anne, he
saw that she was smiling openly. "So?"

"I've been thinking that maybe it has more truth to
it than the reporter thinks," Anne stated.

"Mind your own business," Michael snapped.

"I can't, Michael. You taught me not to."

Michael laughed dryly. "So I did. What was your
opinion of the show?"

"It went off exactly as you planned. Except . . ."

"Except what?"

"I think Alison was somewhat prepared for you to
do something. At least she didn't seem to let your
walking off bother her."

"She's something, isn't she?" Michael asked.

"She must be if you're in love with her."

Anne's words caught Michael completely off guard.
He stared at her for several seconds, his eyes trying to
penetrate the smug look on her face.

"I don't know what you're talking about."

"Of course not. And you always act this way. When was the last time you locked yourself in your office for a week? When was the last time you took off in the middle of a campaign and disappeared for four days?"

Michael shook his head slowly. "I knew I should never have hired someone as nosy as you."

"I thought that had been my biggest asset."

"It was until three minutes ago," Michael growled.

Anne knew he was not serious, but she was unsure of how far she could really go. "Michael, I'm not trying to be pushy, but what I see happening to you is something that's totally out of character."

"I know," Michael admitted.

"Okay," Anne said, "I won't pry anymore. Is there anything else you need for tomorrow?"

"No, tomorrow I do the show straight. That should throw her off stride."

Anne stood and started toward the door of Michael's apartment. When she reached it, she turned. "Flowers, Michael," she advised.

"Excuse me?"

"Flowers. They're beautiful, they smell wonderful and they say a lot. Night," she added as she opened the door and stepped outside.

Michael stared at the place where she had been. Then he laughed loudly. He already had ordered flowers for Alison.

Alison sipped her coffee and watched the small black-and-white television. She had seen three promo spots for the "Afternoon Show," advertising the battle of the century between the new Hepburn and Tracy.

Apparently the television station did not mind plagiarizing the reporter's words. As she finished the cup of freshly brewed coffee, her doorbell rang. Resignedly, she went to it, and when she opened the door, she found a delivery boy with a long, rectangular box.

He handed her the box, smiled and left her standing in the doorway with a funny expression on her face. Shrugging, she went back inside. She gasped when she opened the box and found a dozen long-stem roses nestled in a bed of green. Their soft, velvet petals were fully open, and their deep color sent a chill racing along her spine.

Then she saw the small white envelope. Picking it up, she opened it and withdrew the card. A second later, the card lay crumpled on the floor.

"You won't do this to me!" she stated to Michael's ghostly image. She grabbed the flowers and marched into the kitchen. But the instant before she released the roses into the garbage can, her arm froze.

She could not destroy something as beautiful as the roses, and shaking her head, she opened a cabinet and withdrew her only vase.

After putting water in it, she placed the roses in the vase and set it on the kitchen table. *It's not fair,* she told herself while studying their delicate beauty. Then she glanced at the clock and knew she had to get herself ready for the drive into San Francisco and her second appearance on the "Afternoon Show."

"Round two," she said aloud.

Alison was fully relaxed. They had been on the air for twenty minutes and were in the last minutes of the show. It was amazing, she had thought during the last commercial, how quickly time seemed to speed by when they were on the air.

The atmosphere on the sound stage, from the

moment she'd walked on, had been tense. But she'd been able to maintain a calm front, and had refused to be baited by Michael.

She'd worn another dress today. One that was conservatively cut, but showed off her figure to the fullest. She had also pinned one of the roses above her left breast to remind her of how devious Michael could be.

When the show had started, John Lawson had gone back to the original question he'd asked Michael the previous day, and Alison had sat silently until Michael had finished.

Then, Alison had listed fact after fact, in an effort to show that Michael's examples were nothing out of the ordinary, and for every new invention, whether it was music, movies or any fad at all, there were always notable extremes.

They had argued skillfully in their beliefs, and by the time the first commercial break had come, neither had seemed to gain an advantage over the other. When they'd returned, it had been Alison's turn, and she'd fielded Lawson's next question skillfully.

From the corner of her eye, she saw a sign held aloft. *Four minutes* read the large words.

Then John Lawson shifted in his seat. "We only have a few minutes left, and I'd like to use them to debate another point that Mr. St. Clare brought up before. As our youth get more and more involved with computer games for recreation, what will happen to the future generations when it comes to activities that require interaction? Ms. Rand?"

Alison fingered the stem of the rose, and then looked directly at Lawson. "Computer games were designed to stimulate the intelligence of the player. It is true that most are one-player games, but I do not believe that they induce an antisocial effect on those who play them. In fact, as I had once told Mr. St. Clare, in most cases the effect is just the opposite.

"However," she went on, "in the case of a youth who demonstrates antisocial patterns to begin with, the games will provide an outlet where he or she can enjoy themselves without being made to feel like an outcast."

"Excuse me," Michael cut in. Alison glanced at him and waited. "You seem to be evading the question, Ms. Rand."

"And you," Alison said as her temper suddenly flared out of control, "are a jackass!"

The studio audience burst forth with a combination of applause and hoots at Alison's shout, and John Lawson could not keep the smile from his lips. But before he could say anything, Alison spoke again.

"Please forgive me," Alison said, "but Mr. St. Clare seems to affect me in a most unladylike way."

"I would have thought that the high priestess of Silicon Valley would never let anyone ruffle her feathers."

"And that!" John Lawson declared as he stood between Alison and Michael, "ends this half-hour. Please join us tomorrow . . ." He paused to look at both of them as they glared at each other. "If there is one."

"Off the air," called one of the stagehands.

Alison, her mind still numb, continued to stare at him. "Your interruptions were uncalled for," she hissed.

"But it's all right for you to call me a jackass?"

"I lost my temper. I'm sorry."

"Are you?" Michael asked, his eyes locked on hers, unaware that everyone else in the studio, from the audience who was still in their seats, to the stage crew, were watching them.

"Yes. . . . No!" Alison stated as she stood. With her single word, the studio audience applauded.

"Alison, this is getting out of hand," Michael stated.

"Is it? Why, because you're not in total control?"

"Go get her, Spencer!" shouted a woman from the audience.

Michael held back what he was about to say and glared at the woman who'd shouted. Then he took a step toward the audience.

"My name is Michael, not Spencer. And Ms. Rand is not Katharine Hepburn. Contrary to what you people may think, this is not a movie, and it's not a game. This is real life, and the issues we're discussing affect each and every one of you. No matter what, neither I nor Ms. Rand is appearing for your amusement. We both believe, very deeply, in our views regarding this issue."

Alison, along with the rest of the audience, stared in disbelief at Michael. Then he turned and started off the stage. The audience began to filter out silently, and Alison, her stomach doing funny things, followed Michael off the set.

Why did he have to defend me? she asked herself, wishing he had just left alone. As she entered the Green Room, which fortunately was empty, she saw him opening the far door.

"Michael," she called.

Michael stiffened and then let go of the door. He turned and gazed at Alison as she walked toward him.

"Thank you," she said in a low voice.

"I only said what I felt had to be said. Alison, we've

let this whole thing get out of hand. It's not an issue anymore, it's our own personal fight being taken to the public."

Gazing into his eyes was almost as devastating to her as touching him had been. She fought against the dizzying sensations, took a deep breath and slowly nodded her head. "I am sorry for calling you a jackass," she whispered.

Michael accepted her words at face value. "We were doing well in there today. What happened?" he asked.

"You did what you said I'd done yesterday. You didn't let me finish, and it made me mad."

"I don't think so. It was more than that. I've been watching you, and you don't crack that easily."

"The roses helped. Isn't that why you sent them?" She knew her tone held a challenge, but he'd asked for it.

Michael smiled and shook his head. "No, I sent them because of how I feel."

"I want to believe that Michael, but . . ."

Michael's features went rigid. His eyes narrowed as he stared at her. "Are we going to let one small mistake ruin what we can have together?"

"Michael," Alison pleaded as her heart raced. But her next words were cut off as Michael grasped her and drew her to him. His mouth covered hers too quickly for her to escape, and as they kissed, heat coursed through her. Her arms went around him against her wishes, and even as his tongue met hers, her hands pressed passionately on his back as everything—their arguing, their public fighting and even his deception—faded from her thoughts.

When he finally released her, she found she could

hardly breathe. "Now tell me you don't care about me," he said.

Gathering her wits about her, Alison forced her body to stop its maddening rebellion and to obey her desperate commands for self-control. She pulled away from his touch, and wrapped her arms around herself as if trying to protect her body from his gaze.

"I do care, Michael," she admitted aloud for the first time. "That's what hurts so damned much. I love you, and I want you, but I won't let you destroy me. I won't let you hurt me again!"

"I don't want to hurt you, and I won't destroy you."

"But you have to. You're too committed to this crusade against computer games to do anything less. I can't let you do it. Computers, and the games too, are an important part of many people's lives. They don't hurt, and they don't subvert, unless they're misused."

"But they are misused!" he countered.

"In the examples you've found. Have you looked at the other side of the coin?"

"I've even looked at the edges," Michael stated.

"And you can't find any benefits?"

"No, I can't."

"So," Alison began in a sad voice, "you've just proven that you must try to destroy me."

"Alison, you're wrong. It's not you—"

But Alison, holding her head high, and not allowing the hurt to show, stopped him from speaking. "It's my work, Michael. I'm proud of what I do, and why I do it. Just like you're proud of your work. You're as devoted to what you do as I am to what I'm doing. The only difference is that I was willing to give up some of that devotion for you. I don't think you can say the same about yourself."

When she stopped talking, she gazed at him.

"I won't let you go that easily," he stated, still feeling the impact of her words.

"You have to, Michael."

"Convince me that I'm wrong. Show me, prove it to me."

"That's what I had set out to do this week, but we've ended up becoming a movie script. A bad one at that."

"Then we'll rewrite it," he declared.

"Can we?"

"Let's try. Let's play the rest of the week straight. I'll present my case. You show me where I'm wrong."

Alison continued to gaze into his eyes. Her hopes were growing, and no matter how hard she tried, she could not hold them back. "I'm . . . I'm willing to give it a try."

"That's all I'm asking." He was about to ask her out to lunch but stopped himself, sensing that to push her right now would work against him.

The door opened and several people, talking loudly, entered the room. Without looking back, Alison smiled hesitantly at Michael. "I'll see you tomorrow."

Chapter Nine

Alison sank into the tub and let the sparkling bubbles that floated on the water engulf her. As the heat soaked into her skin she leaned her head against the cool edge of the porcelain and closed her eyes.

It had been a long, exhausting day, and she was glad it was nearly over. After leaving the studio, she had driven back to the valley, and to Tri-Tech, where she had sought an escape by returning to her work.

At the office she had received the accolades from her peers and a warm hug from Allan Worley. "Jackass is too mild a name for him," he'd told her.

Alison had shaken her head at that. "No, he really does believe in what he's doing." Rather than having to be put in a position of defending Michael, she'd gone to her office and closed the door, spending the rest of the afternoon in her own private, safe environment.

Shutting off the outside world, Alison played with idea after idea, pursuing abstract thoughts the way an English hunter chases a fox. But several hours later, the peace she'd found had been shattered by a repeated and abrasive knocking. When she'd finally opened the door, she'd found Allan Worley standing there with a smile on his face.

"I think you'll enjoy this," he'd said, pulling a newspaper from behind his back and holding it up. This headline was bolder than the previous day's, and Alison had stared at it with a profound shock

LOVEGAMES
THE HIGH PRIESTESS VS. THE JACKASS

"Oh, no . . ." Alison had moaned.

"Oh, yes!" Allan had responded. "Listen to this," he'd added as he'd turned the paper and begun to read.

"I'd rather not," Alison had protested, but Allan did not hear her in his enthusiasm.

"'America's premier social critic, a man who has been called America's social conscience, has been called many things in his illustrious career, usually behind his back. But today the woman whom he labeled as the High Priestess of Silicon Valley, software writer Alison Rand, called Mr. St. Clare a jackass in front of thousands of home viewers.'"

Allan had paused for a breath and to flash Alison another smile. "'The Afternoon Show,' on which both were appearing, began smoothly enough in the light of yesterday's debacle, which had St. Clare walking out of the studio. For most of the show, tempers were cool and the arguments were lucid and well presented.

" 'With only a few minutes of air time left, St. Clare interrupted Rand, and Rand bestowed the title of jackass upon St. Clare. The remainder of the show went up like Vesuvius, while the two combatants shouted at each other until the cameras were shut off.

" 'Word from the studio has it that they continued their argument in front of the studio audience, where St. Clare again lost his temper and berated the spectators.

" 'When St. Clare finally left the sound stage, it is reliably reported that Ms. Rand followed him to keep up the argument for quite a while.

" 'As this reporter noted yesterday, their on-the-air battles are most reminiscent of the old Hollywood-style romantic comedies of the past, and I for one plan to watch these LOVEGAMES until the end of the week. But for today, I declare Alison Rand the winner.' "

"They've got it all wrong," Alison had said when Allan finished reading the article.

"So what?" he asked. "It gives us a little advantage."

"Allan, Michael is fighting over his point-of-view. He really does believe that the games we make—and I don't mean just Tri-Tech, but the entire industry—are harmful to the youth of the country. Calling him names won't solve anything. We have to convince him that he's wrong."

"He is!" Allan had stated unequivocally.

"Is he *all* wrong, Allan?" she'd asked. Without waiting for an answer, she'd turned back to the computer, and hit three keys. Then she left Tri-Tech and drove home.

"And that's my problem," she said to the pile of soap bubbles she held aloft a moment before she blew them into the air.

Alison sighed, opened the bath's drain and stood to let the water cascade from her. A moment later she turned on the shower and rinsed off the remnants of the bubble bath. When she finally left the tub, she was feeling more relaxed, physically, than she had in a long while.

Before she could dry herself completely, her telephone rang. Pulling on her long terry robe, she went out to the living room and picked up the phone. She prayed that it wasn't another crank call and was relieved to hear Sally's voice.

"Can't I ever leave you alone?" Sally asked.

"What—"

"Turn on that anachronism you call a television. Hurry!"

Without arguing, Alison put down the receiver and ran into the kitchen. She turned on the small portable, and glanced at the clock. It was a few minutes after eleven.

Then Alison picked up the extension as she sat down at the kitchen table. "What's going on?"

"There's a news report about today's show."

Alison was definitely confused. "You don't get San Francisco stations at Tall Pass."

"I know, but Tall Pass has a satellite receiving antenna. Douglas gets all the stations. Now shut up," Sally said as the newscaster began to speak.

Alison listened as the man introduced the next

story, and a moment later, she saw herself, Michael and John Lawson as they had been that afternoon.

She heard herself call him a jackass, and saw again, his instant reaction to the jibe. Then the picture was gone, replaced by the newscaster.

"And so name-calling ended the second day of what is now being referred to as the 'Battle of the Century.' In a rare, unprecedented move, the remainder of this debate between the man called America's social conscience, and the defender of high-tech, will be rebroadcast after the news, beginning tomorrow night. It does seem that Alison Rand and Michael St. Clare have caught the interest of the public so strongly that this station has been flooded with calls."

"And now," the newscaster said with his plastic broadcaster smile, "it's time for the weather with James Lord. Jim . . ."

Alison snapped off the t.v. "I don't believe it."

"You'd better," Sally advised.

Alison was still staring at the blank television, wondering what she should do. "Sally, is Douglas there?"

"Yes."

"Could you ask him for Michael's telephone number?" Silence was her only response. "Sally."

"Alison, do you think that's wise?"

"I have to speak with him."

A moment later Sally gave her the number. "I can come back tomorrow. Douglas will understand."

"No, Sally. I love you for that, but I have to do this myself."

"In that case, please take care. I'll watch tomorrow. If you need me . . . If you need anything . . ."

"I'll call, I promise."

After she hung up, she leaned back in the chair. She had spent most of the day avoiding any thoughts of Michael and most carefully refusing to think about what had happened in the Green Room.

She had spoken to him honestly—told him how she felt, and her words had come from her heart. But when he'd kissed her, everything she'd been saying, every precaution she'd taken to protect herself had fled the instant his lips met hers.

She had been shaken, but not frightened. She had been saddened, knowing that the man she loved, deeply loved, was so completely her enemy.

She stood and went into the living room and hung up the other phone. Then she went to her desk and looked at the stack of printouts she'd accumulated in her research of Michael.

At the dude ranch, Alison had thought she'd learned a great deal about Michael St. Clare, but when she'd learned of his deception, she had blocked him from her thoughts.

In her research, she had seen the public figure, and the changing patterns that had marked the last five years of the St. Clare organization campaigns. Five years ago, Michael had slowly begun to switch his focus from the large manufacturers who were producing dangerously faulty equipment, to the more philosophical and sociological dangers that faced the population at large.

He had been one of the leading figures in the fight for more public access television, and had loudly deplored the violence inherent in children's morning shows.

He'd focused a great deal of attention on the educational system of the country and had exposed the practice of poorly trained medical students from other nations taking up their residency positions in America.

"So much good," Alison whispered as her fingers traced along the top-most sheet of the printout.

Then Alison dialed Michael's home number. It rang four times before the deep voice filled her ear.

"Michael, did you see the news?"

"Yes," he replied, his voice level.

"It's really being blown out of proportion."

"Maybe it's a more important issue than you thought it was," he ventured.

"I think they're just trying to amplify our personalities, not the issue."

"I think you're right."

Alison held her breath for a moment, trying to restrain her surge of joy at talking with him. "What are we going to do?"

"What we said we would today. Make the people listen to the facts. Present our arguments, and let them decide for themselves."

"Without turning it into a spectacle?"

"That would be nice," Michael said.

"Yes, it would," Alison agreed. Then there was nothing else to be said, but strangely, she didn't want to hang up.

"Alison?"

"Yes?"

"Meet me for breakfast tomorrow morning—"

"Michael—"

"To discuss how we can work out what's best for the show."

Alison wanted to say yes. Her heart cried out for her to say yes, but she knew that every time she was near him, her resolve began to weaken.

"I don't think that would be a wise thing to do," she

said, firming up her voice and her determination at the same time. "Good night," she whispered as she hung up the phone.

Her hand remained on the phone for several minutes before she forced herself to stand and walk into her bedroom. And, as had been happening every night for the past ten nights, a heavy curtain of loneliness fell upon her.

She looked at the bed, and then glanced around the empty room. Taking a deep breath, she refused to heed the call of self-pity. Instead, she slipped between the cool sheets and shut off the lamp on the bed table.

"Go to sleep," she commanded herself.

Wednesday came and went so quickly that Alison thought it had been a dream. The studio audience had the look of a predator watching the death throes of its dinner, and Alison knew that by the end of the show, they, along with whoever had tuned in to see the famed battle between her and Michael, had been disappointed.

From the onset, both she and Michael had responded to John Lawson's questions, speaking eloquently about their feelings, and elucidating their responses so clearly and so simply that everyone was able to understand.

That afternoon, the newspapers had again written a story. The reporter who had been the first to bring notice to the debate had ventured that the calmness was but a front that would surely dissolve the next day. "After all," he ventured, "with two such dynamic personalities, how long can calmness be the rule?"

The reporter had gone on to actually report on

what had been said, and amplified the responses on both sides of what he was now calling an important sociological and educational issue that had been over-shadowed by the electrifying arguments and personal-ities of the debaters.

Alison watched the rebroadcast and by midnight was sure that the next two days would follow the same pattern as today. She had been relaxed on the air and had sensed that Michael was not trying to put her down, but was truly presenting his case as he saw it.

The only problem was that his arguments were too logical, too smooth, and she sensed that if he contin-ued in the same vein, he would prove his point only because he was a more accomplished public speaker than she.

She also realized that she could not fall back on her tactics of provoking Michael into losing his temper. She had to prove that what she was defending was worth defending.

Finally, when the clock read one-thirty, Alison knew that she had to get some sleep to prepare for the next day's show. In her bedroom, she changed out of her clothes and pulled on the long tee shirt that she loved to wear when she slept. She was about to replace the receiver on the base of the phone, which she'd been forced to take off the hook earlier in order to get a little peace and quiet, when her doorbell rang.

Sure that no stranger from the street could have gotten into the building, Alison was angry that one of her neighbors would disturb her this late at night. When the bell rang again, Alison exhaled sharply and went to the door.

Rashly, she opened it and then froze as a camera

flash went off. "Miss Rand, my name is Malcome Gromet of the *National News*. . . ."

Michael was pacing tensely in his living room, trying to find some resolve that would calm him enough to think clearly. The day had been a good one, and he'd been satisfied with his performance on the "Afternoon Show."

When he'd returned to his office, he'd spent several hours reviewing the final reports for a prototype car, which he had given his highest safety recommendation. He had then signed the reports in preparation for his dinner meeting with the manufacturer's representatives and had changed for the meeting and dinner.

Dinner had gone on for two and a half pleasant hours, until coffee had been served. The two manufacturer's representatives, he and Anne Harding had finally left the subject of the new car, and Michael had reluctantly spoken of the debate between him and Alison, when questioned about it.

As he was learning daily, almost everyone was divided in opinion as to who was right and who was wrong. The representatives were no exception. One had sided with Michael, while the other had allied himself with Alison. But their conversation never got out of control.

Then coffee had been served, and as the waiter poured the dark liquid, a man had walked over to the table, swung around suddenly and taken a picture.

"Mr. St. Clare," he said after the blinding flash of light dimmed, "my name is Malcome Gromet of the *National News*. I'd like to have a few words with you about your current debate."

Michael held his temper in check as he stared at the man. "Then I'd suggest you call my office and make an appointment."

"I have, five times, and I can't seem to get one. Give me one now and I'll leave you alone."

Glancing at Anne, Michael saw the slight nod of her head. Then he smiled at Gromet. The *National News* was possibly the sleaziest of all gossip papers in the country. A standing rule in Michael's office was that no interview was ever granted to them.

"I'm sorry, Mr. Gromet, but until this television series is over, I'm not giving any interviews."

"Is it true," Gromet asked, ignoring Michael's even-toned response, "that you have a personal vendetta against the Tri-Tech corporation and are using the power of your organization to get at them?"

"That's ridiculous!" Michael's response sounded more like an expletive than a denial. Although he felt Anne's cautioning hand on his arm, he started to rise to face the man.

Gromet took a step back, but continued to challenge Michael. "Isn't it true that you used coercion to force Alison Rand to debate you?"

"Get out of here!" Michael bellowed, uncaring of the spectacle he was creating in the restaurant.

In that instant, the reporter flipped his camera up and took another picture of Michael's enraged face.

An icy calm had descended upon Michael. He stepped toward the smaller man, his hand snaking out, whiplike, until he grabbed Gromet's lapels and dragged him forward. Leaning over the man, his breathing forced, Michael had spoken in a low, deadly voice.

"Get out, and don't ever come near me again."

Then Michael released him, and the man stumbled backward in an effort to gain his balance.

By the time he had, two waiters and the maître d' had surrounded the hapless reporter and escorted him out. Ten minutes later, Michael and the others had left the restaurant.

And that was the reason for Michael's restlessness. That, and the growing desire to see Alison, to speak to her and to hold her in his arms again.

Then he thought about the reporter from the sleazy newspaper, and his accusations. How had he known about the coercion? From Alison? *No!* He realized that he should have called her and warned her.

Without hesitating, Michael went to his phone and dialed Alison's number, but the line was busy. He waited a moment and tried again. By the fifth attempt, Michael realized that she must have her phone off the hook.

"Damn it all!" he shouted. Without glancing at the clock that read half past twelve, Michael left his apartment and went down to the parking lot. Ten minutes later, he had left downtown San Francisco and was heading into the heart of Silicon Valley.

Alison blinked away the orange dots of afterimage created by the camera's flash and stepped back. But she didn't react quickly enough, and Gromet followed her into the apartment.

"Get out!" she ordered him, shocked and angry at his intrusion.

"I'll just take a few minutes of your time Miss Rand. I have a five A.M. deadline."

"I don't give a damn what your deadline is. Get out of my apartment!"

"Is it true," Gromet went on as if Alison hadn't

spoken, "that St. Clare blackmailed you into debating him on television?"

"Out!" Alison shouted.

"I know it is. Are you having an affair with St. Clare?"

"How dare you," Alison hissed, her rage intensifying.

"You haven't answered my question," Gromet said with a smile.

"And I don't intend to. What I will do," she stated in a suddenly calm voice, "is call the police."

"Before you do, don't you want to respond to my question. I'm offering you a chance to go public with your side of the story. After all, fair is fair. I've just come from St. Clare and you should have heard what he had to say."

Alison's mind whirled. She stared at him and shook her head. *He wouldn't,* she told herself, trying to believe that. "I'm calling the police," she repeated, but her voice was far away as she tried to understand this latest event.

"That won't be necessary."

Alison spun the instant she heard Michael's voice. The reporter paled. That was all he'd had time for before Michael grabbed his collar and half dragged him to the door. At the door he turned back to Alison. "I'll see him to the street."

A moment later, Alison was alone. She sat down on her couch, trying to steady herself. She was still trying to calm down when Michael returned and closed the door behind him.

Without realizing what she was doing, she was on her feet and walking into the comfort and protection of his arms. "Easy, it's over," Michael said soothingly.

Alison shook her head as she looked up at him. "He was terrible. He said that you . . . He said that we were having an affair."

Michael said nothing for a moment. When he spoke, he did not release her. "He's guessing. He was trying to provoke you into saying something—anything—that he could use to sensationalize his story."

"He said he interviewed you."

"He interrupted my dinner and was thrown out of the restaurant."

"Really?" Alison asked as she drew back a little from him.

"Really," Michael said. Then he smiled.

"Do you always answer your door in a tee shirt?"

Then Alison remembered that all she was wearing was the plain white shirt. She had nothing else on at all. She saw again that first flash of light, and as she did a flush began to rise on her cheeks.

"He took a picture of me."

Michael took a deep breath. "I'll see what I can do. Maybe I can get the picture stopped." But his voice held no conviction. "At least that particular paper doesn't get to the stands until late Friday afternoon. We'll be finished then."

"Michael . . . thank you," Alison whispered. She drew completely away from him, aware of how her body was doing crazy things.

"I wish I had gotten here sooner."

Then there was nothing else to say. They just looked at each other. Suddenly, Michael broke the heavy silence.

"Alison, we can't keep doing this to each other. We can't keep avoiding what we feel."

Alison's breath caught. Her heart swelled, but she held her reactions in check. She shook her head slowly, and her voice was low and intense.

"I know that, Michael. But we can't do anything else. We're on different sides, and it's not a game. It's for real. I can't be two different people. I want to be," she admitted truthfully, "but I can't."

"I've never asked you for that," Michael said, reaching out to take her shoulders in his hands. "Never."

"Yes, you have. Not in words, but in actions."

"Then you misread my actions. Damn it, Alison. I won't let you walk out of my life. I can't."

The heat from his hands burned through the tee shirt and scorched her skin. Her insides were trembling, crying out for his touch, but she fought herself and refused to yield.

"Then stop trying to destroy what I represent."

"I don't want to destroy anything! I just want society to see the danger."

"The danger isn't in the games, or in the computers, Michael. It's in society itself."

Slowly, Michael shook his head. "You're wrong."

"And you," Alison said as she pulled away from his grip, "are too stubborn to admit you might have made a mistake. Please leave, Michael."

Michael stared at her, forcing himself to think clearly and to make her understand that their love was more important than anything else. But the harder he tried, the cloudier his mind became. "No! I'm not letting you do this to us."

"It won't work, Michael. Can't you see that?" she cried in a desperate plea.

"No, I can't!" he declared. Then he caught her and

pulled her to him again. He kissed her deeply, passionately, letting all his emotions free.

Alison's mouth met his hungrily, and the suddenness of their passion exploded. His mouth devoured hers, and his arms claimed her for his own. Her heart raced, her breathing deepened, but a lone spark of sanity still glowed in her mind.

Alison grasped at that one spark and clung to it. Even as her heart betrayed her mind, she fought against it, fought to regain the equilibrium he had stolen with his kiss.

Then she felt her willpower growing stronger, even as the kiss deepened and her insides turned molten. *Wrong!* she told herself. *This is wrong.* She knew it was not Michael, or even herself who was wrong; it was the way their battle-scarred emotions were reacting.

Alison tore her mouth from his. "We can't, Michael. Not like this."

Michael refused to listen and kissed her again. Alison stiffened. An instant later she went limp. Her mouth no longer responded to his kisses; her body no longer reacted to his touch.

Michael sensed Alison's withdrawal before he felt her stiffen. Then her warm, soft lips slackened. Her body no longer vibrated against his, and he knew the moment was gone.

His passion, so powerful, fled before this newest barrier she had so suddenly erected. He stared at her, and then shook his head before releasing her and stepping back. When he looked at her, he saw that her face was as emotionless as a plaster mask.

"You're wrong, I'm not the stubborn one, you are. You won't let your defenses down enough to see what really is important. You're too afraid of what you might find." He paused for a moment to shake his head sadly.

"All right, Alison, you win. I won't force myself on you." With that he turned and walked to the door. Alison watched him leave and slam the door behind him. When she was once again alone in the apartment, she slowly, dreamlike, fell to her knees.

"I'm sorry, Michael," she whispered, ignoring the tears that dropped from her eyes. "I'm sorry you don't understand."

Michael had never been as angry as he was when he left Alison's apartment. He went straight to his car, and after he was on the road, he drove without seeing anything around him. The first time he became aware of his surroundings was when he paid the toll on the Bay Bridge.

All his life, Michael St. Clare had never had a moment's doubt about who he was or about what he wanted in life. Tonight he had discovered his first doubt. Tonight he had learned that he was not invincible. It was not an easy thing to accept.

He turned off the bridge and drove toward the wharf. By the time he reached the biggest tourist attraction in Northern California, it was almost three-thirty and the streets were deserted.

Pulling the car to the curb, Michael shut off the engine and got out. He walked over to the very edge of the land and gazed out at the bay. The sound of the water lapping against the cement footings was a quiet contrast to his emotional struggle.

As he replayed the events of the night, time slipped away from him. Before he realized it, the sun was casting its sparkling rays across the waves of San

Francisco Bay, and the next day of dueling was already upon him.

As he readied himself to face Alison, he gathered all the emotions and pushed them behind a steel door he had built in his mind. With one mental wrench, he shut away his love for Alison Rand.

Chapter Ten

Alison's morning was a lethargic haze in which she moved randomly with no one action having any relationship to another. She left for San Francisco at eleven o'clock and by twelve was caught in a freak traffic jam.

By twelve-thirty, she had barely managed to get across the bridge, and at a quarter to one, she'd finally parked her car next to the studio. The next ten minutes blurred together in a race to dress, have her hair done and get into the sound studio. With less than a minute before air time, she was finally seated on the stage.

"I thought you weren't going to show up today," Michael said in a barely audible voice from his seat across from hers.

Today, unlike the first three days of the show, they had both been brought out to their seats ahead of

time, instead of walking out when John Lawson called
them.

"You would have liked that, wouldn't you?" Alison
asked defensively.

Michael raised his eyebrows and slowly shook his
head. "We're here to debate, not fight. Remember?"
he whispered.

It was then that Alison saw the dark shading under
his eyes, and realized that he had slept as little as she
had. Her heart went out to him, but she refused to let
it affect her at that very moment. *I have a job to do,*
she reminded herself.

Then a shout for quiet was heard. A second later,
the activity that had been flowing around them
ceased, and John Lawson smiled at the cameras.

"Good afternoon, everyone. I'm John Lawson, and
this is the 'Afternoon Show.' Welcome to the fourth
debate between Michael St. Clare and Alison Rand.
Now, to begin this segment of the show, I'll direct the
first issue of the day to Mr. St. Clare. . . ."

As he spoke Alison kept her eyes on Michael,
watching the way he sat, moved and even breathed.
When he addressed the issue Lawson brought up, he
did so in exactly the right manner, using his voice like
a sword to make slashing points with every phrase.
When he finished, his mouth curved into a sensual
smile as he looked at her. Alison shuddered with the
memory of how those lips had felt upon hers the night
before.

"Miss Rand, will you respond?" Lawson asked.

"To what?" she asked, unable to stop herself from
lashing out, more against herself than Michael. In that
instant, she sensed the tension in the audience as they
readied themselves to see her and Michael begin to do
battle again.

But now that she had started, she couldn't back down. "Mr. St. Clare has painted a lurid, horrible picture of the results of teenagers playing video games, much the way a preacher speaks of brimstone and fire. But he has still not shown me any valid proof of his claims."

"How much more proof do you need? When was the last time you came out of your sacred cavern in Silicon Valley and walked down a city street? Have you looked at the video parlors? Have you seen the vacant stares and slack-jawed expressions on the faces of your victims?"

Alison's breath hissed angrily. Staring at him, she knew the truce they had declared had been broken too swiftly even to think about. "At least they're not on the street, or in jail for breaking the law because they were so bored by society's demands that they rebelled and did something stupid!"

The instant she'd spoken, she'd known she'd made a mistake. Behind her, several people in the audience applauded, but she was not comforted easily.

"Are you saying that computer games are a deterrent to crime?" Michael asked. She tried to see if he was smiling at her, but saw that his mouth was set in a firm line.

"No," Alison replied. "I was just using as extreme an example of behavior as you were."

"Excuse me," John Lawson interrupted, "but we've got to take a station break." Then he smiled for the camera. "Stay with us, folks, we'll be back after these words."

"You deliberately baited me," Alison stated to Michael as soon as they were off the air.

"You were waiting for an opportunity to attack me," he retorted.

"The hell I was."

"Then stop," Michael commanded.

Alison, about to reply, was cut off by John Lawson. "Save it for the show," he said as he smiled again. "Welcome back. Well, this has certainly turned into quite a battle, hasn't it?" John Lawson smiled again at Alison as he turned toward her. "And now Miss Rand, it's your chance to address a new issue."

"In just a moment. But first I have something to say," Alison told him. Someone in the audience tittered at John Lawson's expression.

Alison faced the audience and drew her shoulders straight. Although she was addressing them, she was speaking to all the viewers. "This debate between Mr. St. Clare and me is a serious thing. But the media has turned it into a circus, and we are all losing our perspectives on what the issue is. And you," she said, turning to John Lawson, "are supposed to be the mediator, not the instigator. Do you think you can do your job?"

The studio was totally silent.

John Lawson was too accomplished a veteran of live television to have been caught by surprise. He smiled forgivingly at Alison, and then directed himself to the audience. "Everyone is entitled to an opinion," he admitted, "and on the 'Afternoon Show,' we have always tried to allow individual expression. Now, shall we continue?"

During the remainder of the show Alison held her temper in check with an iron will, responding to the issues with a minimum of sarcasm and a maximum of honesty. Sooner than she expected, the half-hour was over, and John Lawson was talking about the next show.

"Tomorrow will be the final confrontation," Law-

son said, emphasizing the last word. "The show will
be in two segments of twelve minutes. Michael St.
Clare, as the challenger in this debate, will be given
the first segment to wrap up his arguments and
present the evidence of his findings."

"Ms. Rand will be given the second segment to do
the same. Thank you, and we'll see you tomorrow."

As the theme music played in the background
Alison stood and started from the stage. She did not
look at the applauding audience, nor did she look at
John Lawson or Michael.

When she was safely away from the stage and
locked in the dressing room, she breathed a deep sigh
of relief. But when she stepped out of the dressing
room, she found herself face to face with Michael.

"That was a very noble gesture," he said.

"It was a fact. But thank you," she said.

"Alison, I think it would be best if you and I did not
continue this debate on Sunday at the computer
conference."

Alison studied his face for a moment. "Why?
Afraid of facing me on my home ground?" Although
she had maintained a light tone when she'd spoken,
she saw his hazel eyes cloud momentarily.

"Because I don't think it will do either of us any
good. Let's call it quits in the war department tomorrow."

"And in the real world?"

Michael stiffened when she asked the question.
There had been no lilt to her voice, no hidden
message. Just a simple question. "That ended last
night."

"You—" but she stopped herself from saying more,
as she stared at him.

"All right, Michael," she said at last. Then she

walked away from him, and doing her best not to hear the finality in his voice.

Alison's phone had been silent all afternoon, thanks to the telephone company's finally getting around to changing her number. It had taken them three days. When she'd gotten home, the phone company had called, and after she'd identified herself properly, they'd given her the new number.

She'd called Sally to give her the number and had cut Sally's questions off without any explanation. Then she'd called work, given them the number and made sure that everything was ready for the next day's show.

Allan had assured her that the video tape they had made, along with her special guest, would be at the studio before she arrived.

She closed the curtains, darkened the apartment and pretended she no longer existed. She tried working on the computer but that lasted ten minutes before she gave up in frustration.

She tried house cleaning and made it through half the kitchen before she took an ashtray, reserved for guests who smoked, and threw it at the far wall. She left the shattered pieces on the floor.

Then she tried to read. She picked up a book at random and halfway through the first page tossed it away.

Finally, Alison just gave in to her sorrow and anger. She saw Michael's face in her mind, felt his kisses on her lips and tasted the sweetness of his skin as wave after wave of sadness cascaded over her.

Her love for him was as real to her as anything else had been in her life. She began to understand that the events of the past few days had been nothing more than the offshoot of their entire relationship.

She had been fighting an undefined battle. The real issue wasn't whether games were good or bad; the issue was society's approval or disapproval.

As with their love, Alison saw that there could be no clear-cut victory, but there could be a definite defeat. Michael was a dynamic personality. He was charismatic and his opinions swayed more people than Alison could even let herself imagine.

She had been fighting against him, trying to be a voice of reason against his witch-hunt, and she could only hope that she had helped to somehow soften the power of his allegations.

But saddest of all, Alison realized that having taken a stand against him had destroyed any hope there might have been for love and for a future together. Alison mourned for what she would never have again, and for what she might never be able to give someone again—herself.

Alison watched herself in the mirror as the hairdresser brushed her hair. Suddenly she stopped the woman from continuing.

"Straight back," she said. "The way I always wear it."

"But," the hairdresser began.

"I'm not going to hide behind those bangs today," Alison declared.

The woman obediently dampened Alison's hair and, using a blow dryer, brushed it back. As soon as she finished, the door opened and Alison saw Sally's image in the mirror.

"Oh, no," Sally groaned when she saw the old hairstyle.

"Oh, yes. I'm not going to be someone else today."

"At least you're wearing a dress," Sally commented.

"I'm not totally stupid. What are you doing here?"

"Did you think I wouldn't come after the way you sounded yesterday?"

Alison smiled. "I guess I was pretty bad."

"You don't have to guess. Want to talk?"

"There's nothing to say."

There was a knock on the door, and the assistant producer poked her head inside. "Five minutes."

Alison nodded her acknowledgment. "My video tape is set up properly?"

"You have my word, Ms. Rand. Besides," the A.P. added with a conspiratorial wink, "I'm on your side in this one."

"Is Douglas here?" Alison asked Sally after the woman had closed the door again.

"He's waiting in the studio. We're part of the audience."

"Good . . . Sally?"

"Yes?"

"I tried, I really did," Alison whispered as her eyes moistened.

"I know," Sally whispered.

Alison regained control of herself and took a deep breath. "How do I look?"

"Lovely," Sally stated, wisely not mentioning the dark circles under her friend's eyes that were almost, but not quite, covered by the makeup.

"Thanks for lying to me," Alison said with a flickering smile.

"Anytime. Come on, champ, let's go get 'im."

"Yes, ma'am!" Alison declared, standing quickly and saluting Sally. A few minutes later Alison was being led onto the stage by the assistant producer. Michael was already seated, and her heart skipped when she glanced at the handsome, serious lines of his face.

Ignoring the technician who was hooking up her clip-on microphone, Alison looked past the chaos of the stage hands and glanced at the audience. She spotted Sally and Douglas sitting in the second row and tried to smile when Sally waved at her.

Then she found Allan Worley and half the staff of Tri-Tech sitting in the third section. Next to Allan was a ten-year-old boy who, when he saw her, smiled and waved.

Her eyes skipped around again, and Alison saw several people clustered near the back of the studio. One woman, a tall redhead, stood out among the rest. She knew the woman was Anne Harding, Michael's assistant. Although she had never met her before, she had seen her picture several times in various papers.

John Lawson walked onto the stage, and Alison's attention turned to him. The host of the show was wearing a dark blue pinstripe suit that fit him superbly. When he reached Michael, he shook his hand, then turned to Alison and did the same.

"This week has been a lot of fun, I'm sorry it's over."

"I don't know if I can say the same, but thank you," Alison responded.

"You're welcome," Lawson said as he sat between them. "We've got another minute before we start, and I'd like to get one thing straightened out."

Both Michael and Alison nodded their heads.

"Today is not a debate. Today we play by the rules. Michael speaks first, he has his say without interruption."

"Of course," Alison said, making sure not to glance at Michael.

"The same goes for you, Michael." Lawson waited for Michael's agreement before he continued. "Alison, do you want your guest brought out from backstage or the audience?"

"The audience, I guess," she replied.

"What guest?" Michael asked, his voice tight and forced.

Lawson stared at Michael for a moment. "I thought you knew."

"Enlighten me," he said tersely as he looked directly into Alison's eyes.

"He's not a threat to you," Alison said in a calm voice that she prayed would remain. "He's a ten-year-old boy."

"This wasn't part of the agreement," Michael said to Lawson, feeling uneasy with this new discovery.

"Yes, it was. As I said, I thought you had been told. It was the only way Alison would agree to do the show. Michael, you did ask to debate her."

Michael shook his head, but said nothing further and Alison breathed a sigh of relief. The countdown started.

The last one, Alison said to herself.

The flurry of activity stopped, and silence ruled the sound stage. The time was counted down, and then John Lawson was smiling and talking. He introduced Alison and Michael again, explained the rules of this particular show, and then turned the show over to Michael.

Alison's breath became labored, and her heart felt painfully heavy as Michael spoke. His words were clearly enunciated, and his face was devoid of any humor.

"Alison Rand and I have spent a week arguing, and making no real progress. Today I want to show you exactly what we've been talking about. For the next few minutes, I will talk while a video tape is being played, and I will try to convince you of why these computer and video games are so harmful to our children."

When Michael paused, Alison saw the large overhead monitor flash on. A moment later she was watching a video game in action.

She, along with the rest of the audience, watched the game progress while Michael gave a commentary. At first his voice seemed loud, but soon, it softened as he backed up his accusations with precise facts. He gave the figures of how many games had been manufactured, and how many were sold. He spoke of the amount of money spent in video game parlors, and then continued in perfect sync with the tape as different scenes flashed across the monitor.

Alison forced herself to watch the tape and to listen to every syllable Michael uttered. She tried to find a flaw in his logic, but found it impossible. He was arguing from a position of strength, but it was still a position which did not encompass the whole subject.

When he spoke about the educators who blamed video games for distracting students and turning them away from schoolwork, she could barely restrain herself from jumping up and shouting at him. Instead, she sat as still as death while she continued to listen and watch.

Her own gasp mingled with the studio audience's as what, at first glance, seemed to be a huge caricature of a teenage boy filled the screen. His eyes were wild, and his mouth was half open. He looked insane, and the subversive impact was undeniable. Then the image shifted, and the wild face grew smaller until the boy's entire body could be seen as he played a large arcade-style video game.

Alison felt as though she had been slapped. The trick photography had shocked her, and it had taken several seconds to recover.

"This," Michael was saying, "is what happens when computer games become obsessive toys for teenagers. What you're seeing now is not a staged film, but an actual afternoon at the video parlor. Look at the faces of the kids playing the games."

A powerful, random collage of shots flickered across the screen. Shot from every conceivable angle, the teenagers playing the games looked as if they belonged in a nightmare.

"Violence, destruction and killing are the basis for all these games, and you can see the bloodlust on the faces of the players. The faces of your children!"

As suddenly as the film had begun, it ended, but Michael continued speaking. "I will admit that what you've just seen was very dramatic. But it was necessary to make my point. Computer games are not just toys. They are not just harmless, exciting gadgets of modern technology. They are an ever increasing danger to our children.

"In closing, I would like to read a statement from Dr. Hugh Friedlich, the eminent child psychologist. Dr. Friedlich states that 'because of the lack of human interaction, other than physical response to a given stimulus, computer games can be a serious detriment to a child's development.'

"As you see," Michael said as a card with the thirty-second warning was held up, "Dr. Friedlich agrees with all the educators I've already spoken of, in his belief that video games are indeed a subversive influence on our youth. Thank you."

"And now a word from our sponsor," Lawson said quickly.

As soon as he finished speaking, the studio audience applauded Michael's speech. But Michael, after nodding his head to them, turned to Alison with one eyebrow cocked.

"That was a rotten way to make a point," she stated.

"You didn't like the film?"

"I . . ." She stopped herself, and then smiled. "Listen to what I have to say, Michael. Listen to it. Don't shut it out." Then she turned and looked out into the audience until her eyes fell on ten-year-old Vincent Ramalo.

Faster than she thought it should happen, she heard John Lawson introducing her again. Looking directly at Michael, rather than the audience, Alison took a deep breath and plunged head-first into the current.

"Before I get to the heart of the matter, I want to address Mr. St. Clare, and his eloquent statement. I cannot deny that many of the things you say are true. But as I've tried to point out all week long, nothing is without its bad side. Everything you've said and shown is true, in a limited way. Yes, there are those kids who play video games instead of doing their homework. But that's no different now, than it was twenty years ago.

"No, as much as things change, they stay the same. We've all heard your facts and figures about the drop-out rate in high school, and the large numbers of students who are failing their courses. Now I have some for you."

Without smiling, Alison stared back at the audience. "Twenty years ago, the drop-out rate was two percent higher than it is today. How can it be video games that are to blame for that, if you take Mr. St. Clare's figures to heart?

"Rather than belabor a point that he worked so hard to validate, I will take the other side of the coin, and talk about the benefits of computers and computer games."

With that, she nodded to the assistant producer. "I too have a video tape to show, so if you'll watch the monitors, I'll explain."

A moment later, Alison saw the overhead monitor begin to play her film, displaying photographs of the first generation of computer games.

"These games were the simplest of them all. But they caught everyone's imagination. They were not difficult to play, and for younger children, they were the best possible way to teach eye-hand coordination." Alison paused for a moment as a three-year-old played *Space Invaders*.

"Several highly respected educators, along with many well-known psychologists, have repeatedly stated that video games have no harmful effect on the well-adjusted, normal child. However," Alison said loudly, as a picture of a teenager intensely concentrating on an advanced game, flashed on the monitor, "if you'll note the clock in the background, you will see that this student should be in school.

"This particular student is cutting school so he can play his games. His actions are not considered normal. He is not a well-adjusted boy. In fact, he has no friends in school, and he is on the border of failing.

"This boy is also under psychological counseling for his problem. The doctor who is treating him has unequivocally stated that it was not video games that caused the boy's problem. If there were no video games, then he would have found another outlet.

"But more important than just trying to defend video games, I want you to know what is behind them besides electronics." Alison paused until her video tape caught up with her, and the inside of a video game manufacturing plant was being shown.

"Video games are entertainment, and they are more. They are educational, they are imaginative and they fill a need that many people have for something new and exciting, and those people are not just children."

Again, the monitor reflected her narrative, and scenes of adults as well as children playing games were shown.

"But in order to get this far, in order to be able to allow people to play games of fantasy, someone has to think them up. That's where people like myself come in."

The front of Tri-Tech's modern building filled the screen. "This is Tri-Tech Corporation where I work. Tri-Tech is involved in aerospace projects, and in computer-medical research. Until three years ago, we never designed a computer game.

"I was working on a special research program to enable a computer to assist a neurosurgeon in a rare and delicate form of brain surgery. There were many problems, and a lot of concerns. In an effort to speed up my research, I began to use graphics to implement the computer program.

"What I ended up doing was to set up a three-dimensional grid that resembled a triple-tiered chessboard. Then I remembered a movie I had seen called *Fantastic Voyage*. In this movie, scientists reduced humans and a submarine to microscopic size, injected them into a surgical patient, and then sent them toward the brain to try to clear a bloodclot.

"Because I realized that technologically we had most of the capabilities that were described in the movie, I began to try to figure out a way to use an idea that the movie had given me. I designed a second grid, and then superimposed the image of a human brain on it." Alison paused for a moment as the very grid she spoke about appeared on the screen. "Rather than get too involved in the complicated details, let's just say that I wrote a program that would allow the surgeon to interact with the computer in pinpointing the problem area of the brain.

"That in itself was nothing revolutionary, but we went one step further. The computer aided the surgeon, and using electronic technology, we were able to guide thin electrodes through different parts of the brain without affecting any tissue except the diseased area.

"Up until this particular interactive software program was developed, neurosurgery for certain types of diseases was considered to be as dangerous as the disease itself.

"With the designing of this software—call it a medical game if you will—came the ability for skilled surgeons to help scores of people who previously had had no chance. And," Alison said as the screen changed again, "the first video game that I designed, called *Vincent's Catacombs,* was a computer-animated version of the exact interactive software used for neurosurgery.

"But instead of electronic scalpels, the gameplayer used a joystick which controlled particle and tractor beams to find a lost treasure in the catacombs that, if anyone looked closely enough, was a duplicate of a seven-and-a-half-year-old boy's brain. The treasure was located in the same place as the tumor that had kept the boy paralyzed for two years.

"And so, as you see, there are many sides to computer games, not just Mr. St. Clare's. There are also thousands of teenage boys and girls who have learned to manipulate and utilize their hands and minds in the same way as a neurosurgeon."

Alison paused as the audience applauded, and the camera returned to her. "Oh, yes," she said, as if she'd forgotten. Turning, she looked directly at Michael's face, which was totally devoid of expression. "The game was named after the boy who was the first patient, Vincent Ramalo." Turning again, she looked out into the audience and smiled at Vincent.

"And this young man," she said as she waved Vincent toward her, "is Vincent Ramalo."

Ten-year-old Vincent ran up onto the sound stage and gave Alison a big hug. She embraced him tightly and felt overwhelmed with emotions as she held the boy.

Then she saw the cardboard sign being waved frantically by the stage hand, and a moment later, John Lawson spoke. "I'm afraid that we've run out of time. We'll be back in just a moment."

Releasing Vincent, Alison turned to look at Michael. Imperceptibly, Michael nodded his head. But she saw that his face was expressionless, and his eyes, although they held hers, seemed to be looking straight through her.

Chapter Eleven

$\mathcal{M}$ ichael sat behind his desk, staring at the television set and listening to the news. Off to the side, Anne Harding sat silently on the long leather couch, intently watching the news show.

Spread out on Michael's desk was the afternoon paper, declaring Alison Rand the winner in their week-long debate. Michael agreed that her emotional presentation had indeed been responsible for her coming out ahead. Yet he felt that now, more than ever, he would have to prove to the public that there was a great danger involved in the use of video games.

Focusing his attention on the television, Michael listened to the newscaster. A repeat of part of Alison's segment was being shown.

"Alison Rand, instead of defending the video game industry, and rebutting Michael St. Clare's charges, turned the tables on him today with an emotional and heart-rending look at the benefits of video games.

"The showing of a ten-year-old boy, whose life had been saved by the use of a new medical technique developed by Ms. Rand, which she later turned into a video game, was the single most important aspect of the week-long debate.

"And as Ms. Rand said, her video game has given thousands of our youngsters a taste of what being a neurosurgeon is like. For those of you who were unable to see the show this afternoon, and would like to see the final segments of the debate in full, it will be rebroadcast tonight at eleven-thirty, following the local news.

"And now on the national scene . . ."

Michael pressed the remote control and turned off the set before turning to look at Anne.

"We're going to have a real uphill battle to get back the ground we lost," he commented.

Shifting on the couch, Anne nodded to him, but remained silent.

Michael held up the paper and shook his head. "She really did me in, didn't she?"

"Not really. She just didn't fight your fight."

"Tell me about it." The newspapers had also declared Alison the winner, but refused to discount Michael's position.

A moment later, one of the office workers came into the office with evident nervousness.

"What?" Michael asked.

The staffer held out another newspaper. "I thought you would want to see this," he said. "A reporter dropped it off. He said his name was Gromet, and that you could reach him tomorrow if you wanted to make a comment."

Michael stared at the young man for a moment, and then held out his hand. "Thank you."

Knowing a dismissal when he heard it, the man wasted no time in leaving. When they were alone again, Michael unfolded the paper, looked at the front page and saw the pictures of him and Alison.

Anne left the couch and walked behind him so that she could read the story at the same time as Michael. Afterwards she waited for Michael to say something, but he only stared at the paper.

"I think I'd better call our lawyer," Anne said at last.

"For what?" Michael asked in a rough voice. "Gromet is smart. He makes no accusations, states no facts. The entire article is made up of rumor and innuendo and conjecture."

"But it's so . . . ugly!" Anne stated. "And so many people read it."

"If we call the lawyer and tell him to file a suit against the publisher of this piece of trash, what will happen?" As he spoke he turned in the chair to look at Anne.

"We get a retraction."

"Buried somewhere in the middle of the paper. No, Anne, if we file a suit, all it will do is lend credence to his story. It will give it a validity that they can't get by our silence. Besides, we did use some coercion, even if it was unintentional."

Anne bit her lip at Michael's reasoning, but knew he had not meant it as a rebuke. "It will hurt the campaign."

"It can't do any more harm than I've already done," Michael stated without any sign of rancor.

"Michael, you're being very hard on yourself. We've had setbacks before."

Michael sighed, but said nothing.

"Do you think Alison Rand told him?" she asked thoughtfully.

Michael shook his head immediately. "She wouldn't do that," he stated.

"Have you gone over the changes we've made for your speech on Sunday?" she asked, switching subjects deftly.

"They're fine," he said. "Go home, Anne. It's getting late."

"I don't mind staying, Michael. If you'd like company."

Michael smiled at Anne. "You've always been a good friend, but I want to be alone for a while. Don't you have a date tonight?"

"Well, as a matter of fact . . ." she said with a secretive smile.

"Who?"

"Would you believe John Lawson?"

"I thought you didn't go for those plastic types?"

"I don't. He's different. Anyway, I'll let you know what happens."

"Only the good parts," Michael joked. After Anne had gone, Michael looked at the *National News* and studied the photograph of himself. His face was animated with rage, and his eyes looked deadly.

Then he was staring at Alison's photo. He saw the startled innocence on her face, and the shocked, outraged set of her mouth. The photo had caught her from the waist up, and the plain white tee shirt emphasized the proud thrust of her breasts.

"Bastard," he growled at the byline of the article.

He wanted to call Alison, but he knew that if he spoke to her, or even saw her, his willpower would crumble and he would find himself wanting her and making more of a fool of himself than he had already done.

It's over, he reminded himself. *It's finished.*

In the outer office, Anne Harding went to the card file on her desk and flipped through it until she found what she was looking for. Working quickly, she copied down the address, put the slip of paper into her purse and then smoothed out her skirt. She had a half-hour before she was meeting John at the restaurant, and she wanted to look her best.

A strange sense of excitement infused her as she thought of the handsome television personality. She had known John for several years and had always liked him. Today he had surprised her by asking her to dinner. But her excitement was tempered by the guilt she had not quite succeeded in banishing from her mind. Her threats to Tri-Tech had caused Michael a good deal of harm, personally, and she felt responsible for the trouble between him and Alison Rand. *Maybe I can help him,* she told herself as she patted her purse where she had just placed Alison's address.

Alison had avoided the party that Allan Worley and Tri-Tech had planned for her to celebrate what they considered to be her victory over Michael. Alison had felt no elation at the end of the show, and she had pleaded exhaustion in order to escape the party.

She had left the small group in front of the studio, but had again been trapped by Sally, who insisted that Alison have dinner with her that night.

When she arrived home, it was almost four o'clock, and all she wanted to do was rest. After locking the front door, Alison wandered around the apartment. The emotional and physical fatigue of the past week was catching up with her and making her movements uncoordinated.

In the kitchen, she saw the scattered remains of the broken ashtray she had flung against the wall, and proceeded to clean it up.

She put on a pot of coffee, but when it was ready, she could not drink it. Returning to the living room, she lay down on the couch and closed her eyes. She fell asleep almost immediately, and not even the vision of Michael's face kept her awake this time.

Sally glanced nervously at her watch for the tenth time in five minutes.

"She's probably stuck in traffic," Douglas ventured.

"Probably." Sally responded, but she didn't think so. She hadn't liked the way Alison had looked after the show, and it had only been on Sally's insistence that Alison had agreed to have dinner with them tonight. Knowing her friend as well as she did, she knew that Alison always kept her appointments or called to cancel.

"Maybe I should call her," Sally thought aloud.

Douglas smiled and covered her hand with his. "Are you always this maternal?"

Sally returned the smile with an even brighter one. "Just wait, you ain't seen nothing yet."

"Give her a call if it will make you feel better."

"I think I will." Sally went to the pay phone in the rear of the restaurant and dialed Alison's number. A moment later the electronic computer voice informed her that Alison's number had been changed and was not available.

Sally hung up and rummaged through her purse for the new number. A moment later she realized she'd left it on Douglas's desk at the resort.

After she told Douglas what had happened, he called for the check, paid for the two drinks they'd ordered, and then drove to Alison's apartment.

"I'll wait for you here. If you need anything, come get me."

Using the set of keys Alison had given her a few years before, she let herself in the front of the building, and then went to the apartment. She rang the bell and waited. When there was no response, Sally unlocked the door and went inside the dark apartment.

She found Alison sound asleep on the couch and, after turning on a lamp, bent and grasped her shoulder while she called Alison's name.

Alison woke, exhausted, and fought against the strange feel of someone's hand. Opening her eyes, she saw Sally bending over her. It had been Sally's hand on her shoulder, gently shaking her, that had awakened her.

"What?" she asked, trying to focus on her friend's face.

"It's eight-thirty. We've been waiting for you since seven. I got worried and came over."

It took Alison another few seconds to make her sluggish mind function. Sitting up, she took a deep breath. "Sorry."

"It's okay, I was just worried. I'm glad I had the keys to the apartment."

"Where's Douglas?"

"Downstairs, waiting in the car."

"Sally, I don't feel like going out tonight."

"I can see that. Alison, I just wanted to make sure you were okay."

"I'm fine."

"Are you?"

"Damn it, Sally, I said I was fine. Leave it at that."

Sally refused to be intimidated by Alison's outburst. "Then can we go to dinner?"

Alison sighed, and then stood. "I really don't feel like it," she said.

"Alison—"

"And I'm not shutting myself away. I'm not hiding. I'm just tired, very, very tired. Sally, please . . ."

"And very, very upset," Sally added.

Alison tried to control her temper, tried, and failed. "Yes, I'm upset. In the space of two weeks, my entire life has been turned upside down. First I acted like a silly, lovesick girl, and then I ended up in a battle to save my professional life. And it was all because of one egotistical, self-centered man who can't see anything else but his own point of view."

Sally let Alison's tirade continue until she fell silent. "In other words, you're in love with Michael, but you won't see if you can work things out."

Alison shook her head vehemently. "You're wrong this time. I told Michael that I wanted to work it out after the debate was over. He didn't want to hear that. It was either right then or never. Michael ended it, not me!"

When she finished, tears had once again sprung from her eyes. "Oh, damn it, Sally, I promised myself I wouldn't cry again."

"Why? Are you too tough?"

"No, I'm too tired," she said truthfully. "Sally, except for this afternoon, I haven't slept more than two hours at a time. I feel like I'm about to explode. I hurt, and I can't stop hurting."

"Maybe you don't want to stop," Sally whispered. "Maybe you don't even know that."

"Sally, please," Alison begged, turning her back on Sally.

"All right, I'll leave you alone. Just try to think about why you hurt so much. And while you're at it, think about whether Michael is worth fighting for."

Alison couldn't reply, and a moment later, she heard her front door close.

Sitting back down on the couch, Alison stared out the window at the darkness of the night. With Sally's remonstration had come another wave of painful memories, memories that haunted her with their finality.

For another two hours, Alison stared at nothing while she fought to control her feelings; ever increasing rushes of emotion refused to relinquish control over her mind.

When she was able to stop thinking about Michael and what could have been, she left the living room and went into the kitchen to reheat the coffee she had not touched earlier. When she had a steaming cup poured and was sitting at her kitchen table, she glanced at the clock, and then turned on the small television set.

The news was almost over, and she had hoped that there would be no reports about today's show. Alison watched the weather report, which called for a beautiful weekend, and then saw an unfamiliar face fill the screen.

"My name is Jason Collings, and I am the editorial director of KBKZ-TV. Usually, the station's editorials are given by one of my staff, but tonight I felt I had to speak out for myself. The views I will express are a reflection of KBKZ—television."

Alison stared at the television, not quite sure that

she had ever heard an announcement like that one before. Then, as the man spoke, her stomach tensed again.

"It seems," the editorial director said, "that the Rand/St. Clare debate is now being given national focus by a publication that has a history of exploitation, the *National News*. Today's issue raises the question of the validity of the debates we have been airing, and claims that Michael St. Clare is using the topic of computer games to keep his name in the public's awareness. The newspaper also claims that St. Clare coerced both Alison Rand and Tri-Tech into this debate."

Then the man shook his head sadly. "In my opinion, and that of this station, this is an example of the shoddiest type of journalism. The story is based on rumors and gives no facts to substantiate it. Furthermore, the story goes on to say that not only is the debate a sham, but that Alison Rand and Michael St. Clare are having a clandestine affair.

"For those of us who have watched this debate, we have been made aware of the tremendous effect that computers are now having on the people of this country. And we are also aware that this debate has been able to make people stop and think and decide about the issues for themselves.

"In no way can anyone consider the week-long debate to be a sham. Michael St. Clare is a highly respected man who, in our opinion, has shown time and again that he is not the sort of person to seek media coverage for his own benefit.

"In closing, I ask all of you to once again watch the final show of the debate, which will immediately follow this editorial, and make up your own minds.

For us at KBKZ, we know that these two people have presented us with an honest topic. I wish that the *National News* would do the same. Thank you, and good night."

Alison sat transfixed, her coffee cup halfway to her mouth, throughout the entire editorial. She had known nothing about the newspaper article and was shocked to hear what the man had said.

By the time the commercials were over, Alison had put down her cup and was about to turn off the set, when she saw Michael's face staring out at her as the repeat of that day's show started.

She watched the entire show, feeling like a voyeur, knowing exactly what would happen, how, and when. She experienced the same shocked reaction to Michael's film of the video arcade, but this time she did not feel the outrage.

She saw herself introduced, and watched the video tape she and her colleagues had put together. She heard the deep convictions in her voice.

As soon as her segment ended, Alison shut off the set. She stared at the blank screen for several minutes, trying to recover from everything that had happened. She began to think about what Michael had said. She pictured the tortured faces of the teenagers, and heard his impassioned plea for society to beware.

She forced herself to stop thinking about that. *It's too dangerous,* she told herself. Besides, she thought, she had asked him to hear her side and he'd refused. She wouldn't let herself be trapped by his influence.

Besides, she had to buy a copy of the *National News* even though she knew she wouldn't really like what had been written. Glancing at the clock, Alison saw that it was just after midnight. All the stores were closed, but the *National News* was sold in every grocery store on the West Coast.

Ten minutes later, Alison pulled into the parking lot of a large chain grocery store. Inside, she went directly to a check-out counter and picked up an issue of the *National News*. She glanced at the front page and saw herself, dressed in her tee shirt, looking back at her.

Folding the paper, she paid for it and left the store, praying that no one would recognize her.

During the short ride home, Alison refused to look down at the seat where the paper lay. But once she pulled into her parking space, she couldn't help herself.

Turning on the interior light of the car, Alison picked up the paper with hesitant hands. She looked at her picture, and at Michael's. The rage she saw in his face startled her for a moment, because it made him look like a stranger. But that was the way they wanted him to look, she thought.

Then she read the article, and with every piece of slander, she grew angrier and angrier. By the time she finished, her rage was hardly containable.

She didn't care about the allegations of an affair between her and Michael, especially because there hadn't really been one—just a single beautiful night together before the world had crumbled into reality could hardly be called an affair.

What did bother her, what made her so angry, was that someone at Tri-Tech had spoken to Gromet and told him about the St. Clare organization's coercion. She felt the allegations were directed against her as well as Michael.

She left the car and, taking long, fast strides, went

to the front door, unlocked it and stepped inside. She did not hear her name called, or see the tall redhead running after her. Her entire focus was centered on the article, and on finding out who had betrayed her to the reporter.

Once she was in her apartment, she dialed Allan Worley's number, and waited impatiently for him to answer. When he did, she didn't give him a chance to speak.

"Who told that reporter about what happened between St. Clare and us?" she demanded.

"Alison?" Worley asked in a husky, sleep-etched voice.

"Who, Allan?" She heard his hesitation.

"I'm sorry, Alison. It was unintentional."

"You told him?" she asked, unable to believe it.

"I didn't know who he was. He came by the shop two days ago. He said he was with the software conference, and wanted to get some background on you to use when he introduced you and St. Clare."

Alison remained silent, listening to Allan and trying to rein in her temper.

"We got to talking, and he kept saying how much he admired you and the way you were facing up to St. Clare. Then he said how surprised he was that you, and not someone more experienced in broadcast, had agreed to take him on.

"I guess it was a combination of pride in you, and some leftover indignation at St. Clare, but I told him what had happened."

Alison drew in a slow breath even as she shook her head in denial of what she was hearing.

"But I had told him that what I said was confidential. He'd promised me he would keep it that way."

"Right," Alison said dryly. "He didn't tell more than a couple of million people."

"Alison, I'm sorry."

"So am I, Allan."

"Can we talk about this tomorrow, at the conference?"

"I'm not going to the conference," she told him flatly.

"But . . . Alison, you have to."

"I will not put myself on display anymore."

"They've scheduled you to reply to St. Clare on Sunday. You can't back out of it now."

"Yes, I can, Allan," Alison whispered as she hung up the phone. Then she just stared at it, wondering why she had let everyone else's needs dictate what she did with her life. First it was Michael challenging her; then it was Allan asking her to debate Michael. Then it was Michael deceiving her, and Allan telling her not to debate him. Television had jumped on the bandwagon, and the newspapers had followed quickly behind.

Everyone had chosen a side; everyone was watching to see the blood spilled in the streets. *But what about me? What about what I want?*

Anne Harding had said good-night to John Lawson after several very enjoyable hours. After he'd escorted her to her car, Anne had left the parking lot but had not gone home; she'd driven to Alison's apartment building, ten miles outside of San Jose.

After parking near the entrance, she'd gone to the front and rung the buzzer underneath Alison's name. When her second ring went unanswered, she returned to her car and started it. As she prepared to pull out she saw a car drive into the parking lot. A moment later the car's interior light went on and she recognized Alison.

Anne started out of the car, but realized that Alison was reading a paper. Then, Alison left the car and walked to the building and Anne tried to catch up to her. She called Alison's name, but the woman did not respond.

Anne reached the door just after Alison walked through. Catching the door before it locked, Anne followed Alison toward her apartment.

By the way she walked, Anne knew something was wrong. At the apartment door, Anne paused, her hand upraised to knock on the not quite closed door, but held back when she heard Alison's angry voice.

Dropping her hand, Anne waited until Alison finished speaking and hung up the phone. Only after she digested what she'd heard, did she knock.

Alison spun at the sound of the knock, and recognized Anne Harding immediately. She watched the woman push the already opened door out of her way and step into the apartment. "Ms. Rand," she said.

"Please come in, Ms. Harding," Alison said tersely.

"I usually don't walk in"—Anne shrugged as she spoke—"but you left the door open."

Alison nodded her head wearily. "So it seems. Why are you here?" she asked bluntly.

"To talk with you."

"Why? Did Michael send you with another challenge?"

Anne refused to allow Alison, who she knew was already upset, to make her lose her temper. "I'm here on my own. Please, Ms. Rand . . ."

"Call me Alison. All my enemies do," she said bitterly.

"I guess I made a mistake in coming here," Anne replied in a level voice. "Good-bye."

As the tall redhead turned stiffly and started out of the apartment, Alison realized just how foolish and shallow she had sounded. "Wait, Ms. Harding, I'm sorry."

Anne turned back to her, a shadowy smile on her lips. "No, you have every right to be angry. It's I who am sorry. I came here to tell you that."

Alison shook her head in bewilderment. "I don't understand."

"What happened at the beginning was my fault," Anne stated, meeting Alison's eyes openly. "After the first show that you and Michael were on, he seemed to become obsessed with debating you. He asked me to set something up so that the two of you could debate, and he made it very clear that he would debate only you, no one else."

"Why?"

Anne smiled. "I asked myself the same question, and I couldn't find an answer at first. I called Tri-Tech to set up the debate. I spoke with Dr. Worley, who was more than happy to work out the details of the debate, but preferred to have someone with more experience debate Michael.

"He called me back to tell me that you had declined the offer. But that he would arrange for someone else to do it."

"When I told Michael what Worley, and you, had said, he refused to accept it. Then he asked me to find out where you were. I did, and when he learned you were at Tall Pass, he just walked out of the office and went after you."

"That," Anne said with a shake of her head, "was when I made my mistake."

"What mistake?"

"I called Allan Worley and . . ." Anne took a deep breath. "I told him that if you didn't appear on the show with Michael, we'd target Tri-Tech ahead of anyone else."

Alison could say nothing. She just stared at Anne.

"Michael called me the next day, and I told him what I'd done. I could easily tell how mad he was. He ordered me, in no uncertain terms, to call Dr. Worley and apologize for what I had done, and tell him that we would accept anyone he chose to debate us."

Confusion was replacing Alison's anger—anger at the fact that Michael had known what was happening, to confusion at Anne's last statement.

"But I couldn't reach Dr. Worley, and no one at Tri-Tech would tell me where he was. They would only say that he was not in and was not expected back until the following Monday."

"That was on a Friday?" she asked.

"Yes, I tried to get him all day Friday. Saturday morning, Michael called me. He already knew that I hadn't been able to get through to Dr. Worley. How, I don't know."

Alison, despite the chaotic balance of her emotions, giggled. "Because I dumped a pitcher of water on his head."

Anne's eyes grew wide. "Really?"

Alison bobbed her head quickly.

"Thanks," Anne said.

"Excuse me?"

"I've wanted to do that to him myself. Sometimes he can be so . . . smug!"

Alison found herself agreeing with Anne, and began to warm to the woman. "But why are you telling me all of this?"

"Because I feel responsible for interfering in your life and Michael's. If I hadn't, the two of you would not have spent the week on television yelling at each other. You would have done what you should have, and spent enough time together to realize that love is what the two of you are feeling, not anger."

Alison stayed silent for several long seconds. She stared at Anne, then she sighed. "Thank you for coming here, and for telling me what you did. But as far as love . . . Michael's life and mine are too different. Besides, things have happened that you had no hand in. No, Michael and I are not for each other."

"He loves you, Alison. I've never known him to react to a woman the way he has to you. He loves you, believe me, he does."

"And I love him, but he said it himself. It's over."

Anne wanted to say more, but restrained. She had already interfered too much in their lives, and she would not do so anymore.

"I'm sorry Alison, I truly am." Anne walked to the door, but even as she opened it she turned to look at Alison. "When I came up before, you were on the phone. I couldn't help overhearing you. Are you really not going to speak at the conference?"

"No. I think the people who are involved in designing games should hear what he has to say. If I'm there, it will only incite another argument, and no one will consider the most important thing of all." Alison paused for a moment.

Anne waited silently.

"Someone's right to express an opinion, even if it's not what the people want to hear."

"Alison," Anne said a moment later. "My boss is stupid sometimes, and blind too." With that, Anne walked out of the apartment, leaving Alison Rand to her own thoughts.

Chapter Twelve

Sunday morning dawned with a magnificent sunrise that gave the land a wondrous glow. Alison, sitting near the edge of a cliff that dropped straight into the ocean, wondered why she was unaffected by the beauty that was surrounding her.

Below her, the waves crashed against the rock cliffs which she had been sitting atop since well before dawn. Except for a few lonely cars, this section of the Monterey Peninsula seemed deserted—unusual this time of year.

She had come here to get away, to find some peace of mind and to loosen the tenacious grasp of her unfulfilled wishes and cast them into the ocean. She had hoped that by doing so, she could find within herself some semblance of normality. But as hard as she tried to separate herself from those painful longings, they would not leave her.

Alison had slept only fitfully Friday night, and on

Saturday a good deal of time had been spent in fending off telephone calls from Allan and several members of the conference committee, who had again tried to convince her to attend the conference. Sally had called too, surprised that she had canceled her appearance, but concerned about Alison and not the debate. Before Sally had hung up, she'd told Alison that she understood her not wanting to speak at the conference.

The combination of Sally's talk with her on Friday night, and Anne Harding's unexpected visit, had set Alison's mind following a hundred different trains of thought. In the last thirty-six hours, Alison had replayed her life over and over again. But the one refrain that had kept echoing in her mind was Anne's parting statement. "He loves you."

Yet no matter how Alison tried to make herself believe that, she kept remembering the arguments and the pain. If Michael loved her, truly loved her, then why hadn't he told her so? The debate was over, it was history. Nothing stood in his way.

Alison gave a mental shrug, knowing that even if he had returned to her, it could not have worked. Michael's entire philosophy opposed hers. What she believed in, he did not. What she wanted out of life, she could not picture Michael sharing.

She had once told him that she was willing to give up a part of her life she'd devoted exclusively to work. But she wasn't prepared to give up her work for him. He had not offered anything remotely similar to her.

What had he said? she asked herself, thinking back to the time at the dude ranch. It was something about no middle ground, she thought. *Yes!* "There has never been a reason for me to find a middle ground," he'd told her that afternoon when they had ridden on the mountain. *And apparently I didn't give him the reason to look for one,* she told herself.

The noise of a car's engine caused Alison to turn. Standing, she looked down the highway and saw the first of what would be a day-long procession of cars on the Monterey Peninsula.

Knowing that it was time to go, Alison glanced wistfully back at the ocean before she went to the car.

"We'll be there," Douglas promised. He waited a moment longer and then hung up the phone. Turning to Sally, he shook his head slowly.

"That was Anne. Michael left two tickets for us to attend the conference this afternoon."

"You don't look very pleased."

"Anne said that Michael hasn't left the office since Friday night. He's been totally uncommunicative."

Sally shrugged her shoulders. "Coffee?" Douglas nodded to her. After she poured them another cup, she sat down across from him. "Do you think you should go see him?" she asked, picking up the conversation.

Douglas shook his head thoughtfully. "I've known Michael for a long time. He's trying to come to terms with something that's upsetting him. I remember in college . . ." Douglas let the words fade away. He didn't want to bring back those unhappy memories.

Sally saw the troubled look cross his face and she understood. "That time you told me about . . . the accident?"

Douglas nodded his head.

"Well, then, I guess we'll just have to let him figure it out by himself. Doug," Sally began, but paused for a moment as she gazed into his eyes.

"Hum?"

"Are you nervous?" she asked.

"About today? No, why should I be?"

"Not about today. About us . . . about the future?"

"I've never been less nervous, or more certain," he stated, reaching across the table to take her hand.

Sally smiled shyly, and then blinked the sudden moistness from her eyes. "Thank you," she whispered in a husky voice. "Now, what do we do about Alison and Michael?"

Douglas shook his head and then stood up. He went around the table, lifted Sally from her chair and pulled her into a strong embrace. "It's time to let them figure it out—it's the only thing we can do."

"I love you," she said.

Douglas, taking a line from a very famous movie, winked at her. "I know." Then he kissed her.

Michael, dressed in a somber gray suit, a pale blue shirt and a deep blue tie, pulled out from the parking lot in his building. He had three hours before he was scheduled to speak, and he needed an hour and a half to take care of one very important task.

He'd spent the weekend alone, not in preparation for the conference and the people he would be addressing, but deep in thought about Alison Rand and himself. Although he had tried to banish his feelings for her, he had only partially succeeded. When the debate had ended on Friday, he had been awed by the way she had handled herself.

He had also learned some very, very important facts. Alison had been right in everything she had said and argued about with him. It had taken the sledgehammer effect of her emotional finale to make him understand that there was as much good done with computers as there was harm.

With that knowledge had come another hard-to-accept but inevitable fact. He could not make his love for her remain in the background. He needed her, and he had to find a way to show her that.

But every time they had been together, they ended up fighting, not loving. Although he'd known what he should have been saying to her, his words had always come out wrong.

In the past two very solitary days, he'd looked at himself closely and asked himself what it was that he wanted—what was important to him and what wasn't. This morning, as he again watched the last segment of the "Afternoon Show," which Anne had taped for him, he discovered the answer—the only answer.

Instead of driving directly to Palo Alto and to the auditorium at Stanford University where the conference was being held, Michael crossed the Bay Bridge and then turned toward San Jose. When he drove through San Jose, he did not see the unique hybrid mixture of old Spanish and modern architecture that was part of the city's charm, for the single-minded purpose of his drive allowed him to see nothing except Alison's face.

Ten minutes on the other side of San Jose, he pulled up to Alison's apartment building. He strode through the open entrance, ignored the group of people milling about the pool and took the stairs to the second floor. He stood in front of Alison's door for a moment. Then, without knocking, he took out an envelope with her name neatly written on it and slipped it beneath the door. As soon as that was done, he retraced his path, got in his car and drove toward

Palo Alto and the hostile crowd he would be facing in two hours.

Alison returned to her apartment by nine-thirty, her mind no clearer than it had been when she'd left shortly after midnight. She took a shower, put on her bathing suit and went down to the swimming pool. After claiming a lounge chair, she lay back beneath the warmth of the sun and closed her eyes.

An hour later, the noise around the pool woke her. Sitting up, she gazed at the activity and nodded her head in greeting to those she knew. She watched her neighbors, complete with their boyfriends or girlfriends, enjoying the warm day together.

In an effort to push away yet another wave of sadness and loss that tried to overtake her, she dove into the pool. For all the activity around, it was still empty and she swam several laps. Afterwards, she wrapped herself in a towel and went back upstairs to read the Sunday paper.

The rest of the morning passed smoothly while Alison drank coffee and read the paper. She did her best not to think about Michael, or of the day's conference. At least she had been trying not to, until she found herself staring at a picture of Michael. It was an article about the computer conference that had started yesterday morning.

She read the article carefully, and when she was finished, she had become very, very irritated. The reporter, obviously a man who was in full favor of computers and the offspring products such as video games, had ventured that Michael's reception would be likened to a missionary's demise in the land of headhunters.

"Stupid!" she delcared, slamming the paper closed.

Before she could vent her anger further, the telephone rang.

Answering it, she spoke sharply, only to find herself apologizing to Sally for her brusqueness.

"Do you think we can look for my dress tomorrow?" Sally asked.

Alison had forgotten completely about Sally's upcoming wedding and was embarrassed that she'd been so centered on her own problems. "Sally, I'm really sorry. I promise we'll go tomorrow."

"Thank you. Oh, Douglas and I are going to the show today. Want to join us?"

"What are you going to see?" she asked, thinking that a movie wasn't a bad idea.

"The Cannibal Show. We're going to watch headhunters eat a missionary."

"That's not fair," Alison replied in a low voice after she realized her mistake.

"I know. But Doug and I are going to give Michael some moral support. That . . . that won't affect our friendship, will it?" Sally asked seriously.

"Of course not," Alison stated quickly. "He'll need it."

"If you change your mind . . ."

"I won't," Alison said in a firm voice. After she hung up, she went to pour herself another cup of coffee, but found the pot empty. She rinsed the percolator, filled it with water and then took the plastic lid off the can. When she started to measure out the grounds, she saw she didn't even have enough for two cups.

Shrugging, she picked up her purse and went to the door. Before she turned the knob, Alison noticed a white envelope half inside the apartment.

"Who?—" she asked as she bent to pick it up. A

moment later she forgot about the coffee as she read the note and held the admittance ticket in her hand.

She stared at the large scripted words until they blurred together in a whirling, maddening pattern.

"You self-serving bastard!" she shouted. Then she crumpled the note and flung it from her. She turned and marched into the bedroom, changed out of what she was wearing and into a simple dress. At the mirror, using stiff, angry movements, Alison applied her makeup. In ten minutes, she was traveling along U.S. 101, barely able to keep her foot from pushing the accelerator to the floor.

"Coward, am I?" she challenged, as the note from Michael continued to taunt her with its smugness.

You once called me a coward. What would you call yourself today? M.

When Alison reached the Stanford University campus, her anger had not diminished in the least. She'd fought valiantly to hold herself in check, and to give Michael a chance to present his views to the very people he was challenging.

Besides not wanting to be put on display again, and not wanting to have to look at him and feel the way her heart filled with its loss, she wanted Michael to have a fair chance.

Does he think I'm trying to undermine him somehow? she wondered as she neared the auditorium. Her attention was so sharply focused on her anger that she didn't see the security guard waving her to stop. Only when she passed him did she realize she should have stopped.

She turned onto the drive that went to the back of the auditorium. When she reached the rear entrance, she stopped, got out of the car and walked toward the door.

"Hey, you!" shouted another security guard.

Turning, Alison waited for the man to approach.

"You can't park there. There's a conference going on."

"I'm here for the conference," she said.

"You still can't park there," the guard informed her.

Alison's angered response was irrational. For two weeks, people had been telling her what she should or shouldn't do. This guard was the last straw.

"I can't park there?" she yelled.

"That's what I said."

"Watch me!" she snapped. Turning on her heels, she went to the door, opened it and stepped inside, leaving the frustrated security guard staring futilely after her.

Alison stopped the second the door had closed behind her, and drew in several deep breaths of the air-conditioned air. Then she forced herself to calm down as she looked around.

Ten feet from her, sitting at a small table was William Marcus, the vice president of the Programmers and Authors Guild, and a man she had worked with several times in the past on special projects for the association.

As she approached the table Bill looked up, and Alison saw the surprise on his face. "Allan said you canceled."

"I did," Alison stated.

"Then? . . ."

"I changed my mind," she said.

Bill shook his head slowly. "Why can't anything run smoothly. I spent all day yesterday getting someone to take your place. Now I have to tell him he's not going to speak."

"Let him speak. I'm not going to. I just want to watch Michael St. Clare get what he deserves."

Bill Marcus's eyebrows lifted slightly. "Since when have you become vengeful?"

Alison stared at him. "You mean since when have I stopped being a doormat? Since when have I decided that I'm a person and not a machine?"

"Alison . . ." Bill began, obviously seeing that he'd stepped on her toes. "All I meant was that you've always been so . . ."

"Quiet? So easy to control? So passive?" Her anger at Michael was overshadowing her logic, and although she saw how badly she was embarrassing Bill Marcus, she could not find the willpower to stop herself. Luckily Bill decided the better part of valor was to change the subject.

Looking down, he wrote Alison's name on a piece of thin cardboard, slipped it into a plastic holder and held it up for her. "Sorry," he said. "Go ahead in."

Alison nodded sharply, took the badge and, as she walked toward the far doorway, pinned it to her dress. When she opened the door, she found herself at the edge of the stage. Pausing, she looked at the podium and saw a man she did not recognize speaking to the audience.

Then she scanned the audience, and her breath caught. The auditorium was filled to capacity. There wasn't an empty seat in the place. Alison realized that this was a first. At the last two conferences, the speakers had been lucky if they'd addressed a third of the attendees of the conference.

She knew Michael St. Clare was the reason for the full house. As she glanced at the hostile expressions on the people's faces she knew that she was not alone in her anger.

To Alison's left a set of steps led down to the audience. The speaker was going strong, and as he made a loud point Alison slipped from the doorway and walked down the steps. When she was on the floor, she walked to the side and leaned against the wall.

It was ten minutes before two. Ten minutes before Michael would stand before three thousand hostile people—her people.

Michael had been sitting in the second row of the auditorium for a half-hour. Anne was on his left, and next to her were Douglas and Sally. Instead of waiting backstage until his turn to speak, he'd decided to sit among the audience.

He wanted to gauge the atmosphere from up close. Stepping from the audience would also give him a slight edge; when the M.C. called his name, everyone would look for him to walk on stage from the side.

All around him, he had been hearing whispered conversation, as the people began to anticipate his arrival. The slurring, heated comments that flew through the auditorium, and the whispered, almost gleeful anticipation, was like a heavy cloud hovering above them all.

Then, ten minutes before he was supposed to go on, he caught a movement at the side of the stage. Glancing quickly at the side door, he saw Alison step out. Suddenly, a hot band seemed to wrap around his chest. His emotions flipflopped, and then he relaxed as a shadowy smile graced his lips.

For all her beauty and grace, he saw that her features were as rigid as her body was stiff. He had indeed made her angry enough to show up. *So beautiful,* he thought as he watched her walk down the steps and then go to the side wall nearest him.

Anne, who had always been in tune with Michael's ways, had felt as though he'd become a stranger during the last few days. Today, instead of Michael's usual relaxed carriage, she'd sensed his tension. She knew too that it had more to do with Alison than with the conference.

This wasn't the first time Michael had faced a hostile crowd in his career. She knew it wouldn't be the last time either.

Because of the change in Michael, and his insistence that they sit in the audience, Anne had kept a surreptitious watch on him. When she saw his head turn slightly to the side, and saw the muscles of his neck tense, she glanced in the direction he was looking and saw Alison. She wondered what Alison was doing there in light of their conversation on Friday night. But when she saw the ghost of a smile on Michael's lips, she knew that he was somehow behind it.

Without seeming to, Anne tapped Sally on her knee and then motioned with her head in Alison's direction. She heard Sally's audibly deep-drawn breath.

"Oh-oh," Sally whispered louder than she'd meant as she took in the angry set of Alison's small mouth, and the defiant brace of her shoulders.

As she leaned against the wall, Alison tried to think rationally for the first time since she'd read Michael's note.

Suddenly the speaker at the podium finished and, amid a scattering of applause, left the stage.

The M.C. came out and, with a calculated sense of timing, spoke into the microphone.

"We all know that over the last few weeks, the question of video and computer games has been a highly visible subject in the media. Before I introduce our next speaker, I would like to remind everyone that this subject is not a new one.

"Ever since the video games caught the public's fancy, there has been a raging debate over the benefit, and the harm, to society, primarily the youth of our country.

"Video games have their supporters and their detractors. Both sides of the issue have a right to express themselves, and give their opinions."

Alison nodded as he spoke, and then looked around the auditorium. She saw more faces than she cared to admit to, who looked unforgivingly at the speaker as if to say, "Whose side are you on?" Alison didn't like the looks, especially since she knew so many of the people who were staring harshly at the stage.

"In the week that just ended, a debate between Alison Rand, a software writer and a member of our organization . . . " Before he could continue, a wave of applause and whistles greeted Alison's name. The M.C. paused until the sound died down.

"And," he went on in a loud, amplified voice, "Michael St. Clare"—Michael's name elicited a short round of boos and catcalls, but the M.C. acted as if he had not been interrupted— "took place and was aired on local television. Before that, Mr. St. Clare had agreed to speak to our membership, to give his views on the effect of computer games on youth. So now, please welcome Michael St. Clare."

The M.C. began to clap, but at the same time, a strange hush fell over the auditorium. Not a single person applauded, not a person spoke, as every eye went to the side of the stage from where they thought Michael would appear.

Alison, her heart racing, waited for Michael to walk out. Then she heard some people standing up near her and turned as Michael passed them and stepped into the aisle near her.

Her body tensed and her breath was suddenly trapped in her lungs. Michael was standing three feet away; a shallow smile was on his lips. He didn't speak, but he nodded slightly as he passed her and went up the steps she had walked down minutes before.

"I'm not a coward," she whispered as he climbed the steps. Alison's breath returned but her heart refused to slow its frantic beating. She watched him walking with the grace of a mountain lion, standing straight, accenting his height with the flair of his walk.

His curly, somewhat unruly hair glistened under the lights that flooded the stage. His hands, she noticed, were rock steady, and his face was even more incredibly handsome than she had remembered.

The anger that had been sustaining her, giving her the strength to watch him be destroyed by her colleagues, was slowly draining away, and she started to feel the onset of nervous anticipation, and the fear that somehow Michael would be hurt by the time he was finished.

Alison did her best to listen to what Michael was about to say. The audience was still as silent as when Michael had been introduced.

Michael looked out at the audience, taking his time as he gazed at the hostile faces before him. His eyes went from right to left until they reached hers. Although she was a good thirty feet away, she thought she saw a glint flash out at her from within those hazel depths.

And then Michael spoke. Alison shivered at the first sound of his amplified voice. Forcefully, she reminded herself that she was mad at him, and drew upon the fresh memory of that anger to hold her straight and listen to his speech. Suddenly she was able to concentrate on what he said, and not on who he was.

She listened intently and was soon lost within the smooth words that flowed from Michael's too sensual mouth, the very mouth she had dreamed of kissing so passionately every night for the past week.

"You all know me for what I am, an advocate for consumer rights and a sociologist who strives to educate society. I also want you to know that I am not here to condemn you for the games that are having such a strong effect on the public," Michael said, "nor am I accusing you of being responsible for what is happening to the people who get caught up in those games." He paused for a moment to let his words sink in.

Alison realized how different his views were from those he had been espousing all week. *Does he mean it?* she wondered.

"What I am saying is that the games do have an inherent danger. They can become an all-consuming passion for those young people who have not learned how to interact with their peers. They can cause withdrawal from the world as the users strive to become part of the fantasy that you have created for them."

This time Michael had to pause for the response the crowd was so suddenly hurling at him. Shouts of denial sprang from every corner of the auditorium.

People were standing, some holding their fists high in defiance.

Alison watched Michael, his face impassive as he weathered this storm. When the noise began to diminish, Alison saw him lift the sheets of his speech, and as he stared at the audience he crumpled them and let them fall to the floor. Again, her breath caught as she sensed his determination to be heard.

"You can yell at me all you want. You can deny everything I say, but you won't always be able to shut off what I, and others like me believe in. You people are like cloistered monks who have locked the outside world away. From the safety of what you call Silicon Valley, you view the world through electronic circuitry and computer monitors. You have created your own world, and as with every form of society, you consider yours to be infallible. Well, it isn't!"

Alison stared at him. This time the roar that greeted his statements carried an ugly undercurrent. The people were reacting not to what he was saying, but to what Michael represented. Suddenly, Alison was looking at these people as if they were strangers.

"Please," Michael called, "I'm not here to chastise you, or even to tell you that what you're doing is wrong. I'm only trying to make you see the long-range results of your creations as a whole, and to ask you to find a way to control what you've created."

Again the roar increased, but Michael tried to ignore it. He knew he had lost the crowd, but he refused to give in.

"Go home!" shouted one man in the first row. "Get out of here!" The lone cry was picked up by others throughout the auditorium until the noise level was almost intolerable. Yet Michael did not leave the podium.

"No, I won't go home!" Michael replied.

Alison gasped at this as she saw Michael's features harden and the challenge flare in his eyes. Her own heart swelled with pride at his bravery.

"I didn't ask to come here. You people invited me here to speak! So you'll damn well sit back and hear what I have to say."

Silence fell quickly. Many of those who had been standing and shouting abuse at him sat, but scores of others remained on their feet.

"Collectively, you people in this room are the cream of the crop of computer wizards. You are in the forefront of the next century—a century that I'm sure will be dominated by computers. But you also have to think about humanity's needs during the coming years as well as technology."

"We're not stupid," shouted someone from the center of the auditorium. "We know what we're doing." With that, the crowd cut loose again, shouting Michael down every time he tried to speak.

Alison watched the crowd and felt a shiver pass along her spine. When she looked back at Michael, she saw that he was standing bravely, waiting for the noise to ebb so he could continue. But she also heard, in the ugly cries of the people, that they would not listen to anything else he said.

Her anger flared again, and began to burn within her. In that moment her emotionally clouded thoughts cleared, and the truth emerged. No matter what he had done to her, she realized, she loved him. She accepted this, even as she accepted the fact that they would never be together.

Looking across from her, she saw Anne Harding sitting next to Sally and Douglas. Concern was written plainly on all three faces, and hopelessness was reflected as well. Without another thought, and with a new rage that was so totally different from anything she had ever felt before, Alison walked to the steps, climbed them and started toward the podium.

As soon as the crowd saw her, they began to call her name. By the time she reached the podium, the tension in the auditorium was as thick as smog. Several people shouted for Michael to leave, while others called for Alison to tell Michael off.

When she stepped to his side, she looked up into his face. His features were set in serious lines, but his eyes, as they roamed her face, were two questioning orbs.

She gazed at him for several seconds, and then turned to the crowd. Bending the microphone lower, she took a deep, preparatory breath.

"Enough!" she shouted. By the time the echo of her single word faded, the auditorium was once again silent. "You make me ashamed to be a member of this organization. You make me sick with your hypocrisy and your unfairness.

"Michael St. Clare has come here today to express his views. Not to be treated with a disgusting display of immaturity and animosity.

"I have spent the last week defending a profession, and a group of people I believed in and respected. People whom I thought were intelligent, warmhearted and my friends. Now I'm not so sure." Alison paused for a moment to let her words sink in, but she could not hold back the fury that had propelled her onto the stage.

"Why won't you listen to what he has to say? Try to hear what he's telling you? There are more views in the world than just our own, and we might learn something if we listen. Or are you too afraid that some of the things he's saying may be right?

"Well, I'll tell you all something I've learned this week. And I learned it from Michael St. Clare. There is more than one side to an issue, and usually more than two. Everything that has been said against what we do has a basis in fact. You can't have something that's all good, just as you can't have something that's all bad.

"I think all of us should take a good look at what we're doing. Maybe we should see if there's a way that we can help those people who are affected by the work we do. Consider all the problems involved, and what can be done to counterbalance the bad!"

As she glared out at the audience, she searched the crowd, looking for any hint of understanding, but one face blurred into another, and all she could hope for was that they might be listening to her plea.

The silence continued, broken only by an occasional cough, and she finally turned to Michael. Bending, she retrieved his crumpled speech, opened it, smoothed it out and set it on the angled top of the podium. "Please, talk to them."

Michael had been caught up within the power and feelings of her speech, and when she had finished, he just gazed at her. His eyes flickered over her face, and he forgot, for the moment, the three thousand people who looked on. His pride swelled with the knowledge that everything he had ever thought about her had been right.

"Thank you," he said. Stepping up to the rostrum, Michael looked down at his speech. When he looked up again, he saw that the people were watching him, and the atmosphere was no longer so highly charged.

"I don't know if I can say what I had intended to with any more clarity than the words Alison Rand has just used. But I can truthfully state that in the past week, I have learned a great deal about the people behind computer games, and I have discovered, as Ms. Rand herself admitted, that there are more sides to an issue than just my own." When Michael paused, he heard the door at the far end of the stage close.

Looking at the now attentive, silent crowd, he continued. "All I can do is caution you about the results of your work. To paraphrase a somewhat famous person, from your own Silicon Valley, 'Ten percent of the population can effectively control the other ninety percent.'" Michael stopped for a moment to meet the eyes of his audience. "This is done by example. But of those ninety percent who follow the leaders, a small percentage will be hurt. Please, just think about that."

Michael stepped back from the podium. "Thank you," he added.

Chapter Thirteen

*A*lison left the stage as Michael's opening statements filled the air. With each step she took, the rage that had galvanized her into action faded. When she reached the sanctity of the hallway, Bill Marcus was waiting there for her.

"Alison, thank you," he began, but Alison shook her head at him.

"That was so unfair," she said. When Bill tried to say something else, Alison walked past him and stepped outside into the bright afternoon sunshine.

When she started toward her car, she froze, her muscles paralyzed by the scene unfolding before her eyes.

"No!" she screamed as she started forward again.

When she was at the curb, she glared at the security guard who was overseeing the tow driver as he hooked up her car to the tow truck.

"Hold it!" she commanded in a harsh voice.

The guard ignored her as the driver winched up the front end of the car.

"Stop it right now!" she demanded, her anger growing stronger as she glared at the man.

"Look, miss," he said, his grin not quite gone, "read that sign." The security guard pointed to a sign behind her, and as she turned and read it, she shook her head in disbelief. The sign was simple and to the point. NO PARKING—TOW AWAY ZONE.

"You can't do this to me. Please . . ."

The guard's smile grew wider. "Watch me," he said, flinging her earlier, thoughtless words back at her. As if to add insult to injury, the tow truck pulled noisily away from the curb.

"You can claim your car at campus security." With that, the guard walked away, happily humming a tune.

Alison watched helplessly as her car disappeared from sight, and was unaware that someone had come over to her. "Couldn't you stop them?" Sally asked.

Alison turned to her friend, acceptance written on her face. "I deserved it," she said. Then, uncharacteristically, she began to laugh.

But a moment later, when her laughter ended, she saw Sally's concerned, serious look. "That was a very nice thing you did in there."

Alison shrugged. "I hadn't intended to. I had come to watch him suffer, to let him see what it was like to be ridiculed."

"What happened?"

"I got mad. How dare anyone do that to the man I love!"

"Alison," Sally said, her tone one of patience about to shatter, "either you love him and want to be with him, or you don't. But please, make up your mind!"

Alison nodded slowly. "Sally, I didn't mean to drag you into this. Besides, what happened today won't change anything. Michael and I . . ." But she stopped what she was saying the instant the auditorium door opened and Michael stepped out. "I . . . I have to go," she said as her heart began to beat loudly.

She turned and started walking swiftly away.

"Alison, you can't walk home. It's fifteen miles," Sally yelled.

But I can't stay here either, she replied silently.

Alison almost made it to the edge of the first long drive before the car pulled up next to her. Glancing sideways, she saw Michael's smiling face.

"Go away!" she shouted.

Michael sped up and passed her. Strangely, Alison felt a combination of relief and sadness at the same time. But before she could even think about it, Michael stopped his car, got out, and opened the passenger door. A moment later he was leaning against the rear fender and gazing at her.

Alison stopped dead in her tracks, fifteen feet from him. "Leave me alone."

"I can't," he said.

"Please, Michael."

"No!"

Alison drew in a deep breath and started forward, determined to walk by him. Michael straightened up and blocked her path. Alison sidestepped in her effort to get around him; Michael sidestepped and blocked her. Again Alison tried to get by; again he prevented her from doing so.

He stared at her, his arms crossed over his chest, his face impassive. "Let me drive you."

"Let me walk in peace."

"Alison, let me drive you so I can thank you for what you did."

"It's your fault I'm walking!" she said suddenly.

"My fault?"

"Yes, damn it! If you hadn't gotten me so angry, I wouldn't have parked my car in a tow away zone."

Michael nodded his head in agreement. "That's about as logical as anything else that's happened in the last few weeks. . . ."

"You knew I'd come when you left the note," she challenged, unwilling to give in at all.

"No, I only hoped that you would. Alison, I wanted you there more than anyone else. I wanted you to hear what I had to say. I needed you to see that I have been listening to your side, and that you've made me see things in a new way. But I hadn't planned on your rescuing me," he added with a half-smile.

Alison stared at him in disbelief, afraid to trust what he was saying, and afraid not to. "I'm not a coward, Michael."

"I never thought you were. And neither am I."

"I know. I was wrong then, and . . . I apologize, but it doesn't change anything."

"Then why did you come?"

"I told you, because I was mad at you."

"Why?"

Alison exhaled sharply in frustration. "Please, Michael, this is pointless. Let me get by."

"Answer my question."

"I don't have to," she told him. Then she glared at him. "If you don't understand why, then it can't possibly make any difference."

"Oh, I understand, Alison. I understand a lot. And one of those things I understand is that you love me. It's just that simple."

Alison covered the shock and the hurt of his words, because she realized the hopelessness of the entire situation. Then she smiled. It was a sad smile, a smile that said much more than she wanted it to. "Like the very things we were arguing about, Michael, there's always more than one side."

"And you don't think I love you, is that it?"

Alison stared at him for several long moments. Her voice was level, and as unemotional as she could make it.

"No, Michael, I believe you do love me. But I don't think you love me enough. And . . ." Her throat tightened painfully, cutting off her words. Taking another breath, she forced herself to continue. "And I won't accept a relationship where work comes before love. Where one person has to sacrifice dreams for the other. I have a lot to give, but I need just as much in return."

"Now," she said a second later as she fought off another wave of harsh emotions that had come with the baring of her soul, "May I please leave?"

"No," he whispered. "You have no idea how much I love you, but it's time you learned. I love you enough to know that no matter what happens from this minute on, I want to be with you. I love you enough to ask you to marry me, and to spend the rest of your life with me. Is that enough?"

Alison took a step back as she tried to adjust to what he'd said. Her heart beat madly in her chest; her head spun in dizzying circles. She gazed at him, her eyes seeking the truth of his words. "And what about your work?"

"What about it? It's my work."

"Exactly," she whispered. "And you've already

told me that you don't believe in finding a middle ground."

"That's right," Michael stated.

"And I won't give up on what I believe in, not even for love."

"Alison, if you did, you wouldn't be the person I love."

"Thank you," she said, drawing her shoulders straighter and starting away from him. She took one step before his hand fell on her shoulder, halting her and then spinning her to face him.

"Will you stop running away from me!" he shouted.

"Don't raise your voice to me!"

"Then listen to what I have to say. Or aren't you the same woman who just told three thousand people to open their ears and minds and hear what I was saying?"

"That's not fair."

"Who said anything about fairness. Damn it, Alison, I won't let you go again."

"Why?"

"Because I can't! Alison, I told you that there was no place for middle ground in my life. There isn't. Everything I do, I do to the fullest of my abilities, whether it's working, or loving. And I love you. I can keep my work separate from my love. I can leave it at the office . . . if I have something better to go home to. Do you understand that?"

He shouted the last part of his question loudly enough to make a half-dozen pedestrians stop to look at them.

The air was heavy between them as they glared at each other without speaking. Then Michael took another breath. "Well?"

"Well what?"

"Do you understand?" Again, Michael's voice rose.

"Yes!" Alison shouted back.

"Then get in the car!"

"Don't give me orders! And stop yelling at me!"

Michael exhaled sharply. "Please," he said in a barely controlled voice, "get in the car."

"Why?" she asked, her voice almost frozen in her throat.

"No more!" Michael stated. He pulled her to him, and an instant later, his lips were on hers in an explosive kiss that shook Alison to the very foundation of her being. Her legs trembled, and her heart threatened to stop. She thought she was going to pass out, but the heat of his mouth on hers brought her back to her senses.

When they parted, he looked down at her. "The car?"

"I can't," she whispered.

"Now why?"

"My legs aren't working."

Before the last word was out, Michael scooped her from her feet and went to the car. Thirty seconds later, Alison was pressed into the back of the seat as Michael accelerated the car along the road.

"My car!" Alison exclaimed.

"We'll get it tomorrow."

"Where are we going?" she asked hesitantly.

"Home," he stated.

Alison didn't argue with him as his hand took hers and squeezed it gently.

The drive to San Francisco was as blurry as an ethereal movie. Alison's mind kept spinning, constantly replaying the strange confrontation that they'd just had. The strength and warmth of Michael's hand seemed to be the only reality in the world.

But when Michael pulled into the garage of his building, the world came back into too sharp a focus. He helped her out of the car, and then started walking toward the elevator.

"Michael," Alison said as she slowed their pace.

Michael stopped and looked at her. A gentle smile was on his face as he waited for her to continue. "I'm afraid . . . afraid of what may happen."

Michael nodded his head slowly. "So am I," he admitted. "But I'm more afraid of not finding out."

With that, he squeezed Alison's hand and they finished the walk to the elevator. Five minutes later, they were inside his apartment and high above the city.

The ride up had been made in silence, and that very silence continued as Alison looked around the apartment which was so much a reflection of the man with its unconventional mix of pastels and earth tones.

"Drink?" Michael offered as he watched Alison looking around. She shook her head. Then he was next to her again, looking deep into her eyes.

Slowly, Michael lowered his lips to hers, and at the same time, Alison raised herself up to meet him. Their mouths joined, and their arms encircled each other. The kiss lasted for a long time, and when it ended, their breathing was loud in the silence of the apartment.

Alison, her head spinning from the effects of the kiss, and of the day itself, took a trembling breath as reality reared its logical head and reminded her of what had already happened once to them. "Michael, we . . . we have to talk."

Michael studied her face, and kept his hands around her. "Talk," he told her.

Alison escaped from his arms and walked several feet away from him. She clasped her hands together to stop them from trembling.

"You said that you loved me. You even spoke of marriage. Are you sure?"

Michael sighed, but he did not let her question affect him the way it might have before today. He had learned from his mistakes.

"I love you, Alison, and I intend to make you my wife just as soon as humanly possible. We've made a few mistakes, and we came close to losing each other. I don't ever want to take that kind of chance again."

His words warmed her heart, and Alison accepted them fully. "I love you, Michael," she whispered as she willingly returned to where she wanted to be—in his arms.

Then they half-walked, half-floated across the apartment and into another room. Above them, a skylite illuminated everything with the pure light of the sun, but neither Michael nor Alison saw the beauty of that light, all they saw was each other, all they felt was each other as they ever so slowly undressed.

As if their minds had become one, Michael and Alison lay down on the bed together, their bodies met, their limbs entwined, and they did become one.

Alison looked out at the skyline of San Francisco, its lights glittering against black sky like a multifaceted jewel. The sky was dark and pleasantly cloudless; the moon had not yet risen to fill the void with its haunting and beautiful light.

Turning, Alison pulled the robe tighter around her, and then walked across the room to the man who awaited her. Her happiness seemed complete, yet she could not shut away that one last nagging doubt.

"Are you sure you can separate your work from . . ." she began, but the words failed her. She gazed at him, and saw he was waiting for her to continue. "Oh, Michael, are you really sure that there's room enough for more than work?"

Michael gazed at her, his eyes caressing her face even as his hands rose and stroked her cheek. "There is now, and I promise there always will be."

He kissed her, not with the wild passion that had always seemed to dominate their relationship, but with a gentle, loving tenderness that left no doubt as to the truth of his words, or the wonderful future that awaited them both.

SILICON VALLEY IS THE NAME, NOT OF AN ACTUAL VALLEY, BUT OF AN AREA IN CALIFORNIA—OUTSIDE OF SAN FRANCISCO—THAT COMPRISES MANY COMMUNITIES, AND WHOSE BUSINESS PRODUCTS ARE IN THE INDUSTRY OF HIGH TECHNOLOGY.

AND, AS AN ADDED BIT OF INFORMATION, NOT ONE DROP OF SILICON HAS EVER BEEN MINED IN SILICON VALLEY.

MONICA BARRIE
SPRING VALLEY, NEW YORK

WIN

a fabulous $50,000 diamond jewelry collection

ENTER

by filling out the coupon below and mailing it by September 30, 1985

Send entries to:

U.S.
Silhouette Diamond Sweepstakes
P.O. Box 779
Madison Square Station
New York, NY 10159

Canada
Silhouette Diamond Sweepstakes
Suite 191
238 Davenport Road
Toronto, Ontario M5R 1J6

SILHOUETTE DIAMOND SWEEPSTAKES ENTRY FORM

☐ Mrs.   ☐ Miss   ☐ Ms   ☐ Mr.

NAME _____ (please print)

ADDRESS _____ APT. #

CITY _____

STATE/(PROV.) _____

ZIP/(POSTAL CODE) _____

RTD-A-1

RULES FOR SILHOUETTE DIAMOND SWEEPSTAKES

OFFICIAL RULES—NO PURCHASE NECESSARY

1. Silhouette Diamond Sweepstakes is open to Canadian (except Quebec) and United States residents 18 years or older at the time of entry. Employees and immediate families of the publishers of Silhouette, their affiliates, retailers, distributors, printers, agencies and RONALD SMILEY INC. are excluded.

2. To enter, print your name and address on the official entry form or on a 3" x 5" slip of paper. You may enter as often as you choose, but each envelope must contain only one entry. Mail entries first class in Canada to Silhouette Diamond Sweepstakes, Suite 191, 238 Davenport Road, Toronto, Ontario M5R 1J6. In the United States, mail to Silhouette Diamond Sweepstakes, P.O. Box 779, Madison Square Station, New York, NY 10159. Entries must be postmarked between February 1 and September 30, 1985. Silhouette is not responsible for lost, late or misdirected mail.

3. First Prize of diamond jewelry, consisting of a necklace, ring, bracelet and earrings will be awarded. Approximate retail value is $50,000 U.S./$62,500 Canadian. Second Prize of 100 Silhouette Home Reader Service Subscriptions will be awarded. Approximate retail value of each is $162.00 U.S./$180.00 Canadian. No substitution, duplication, cash redemption or transfer of prizes will be permitted. Odds of winning depend upon the number of valid entries received. One prize to a family or household. Income taxes, other taxes and insurance on First Prize are the sole responsibility of the winners.

4. Winners will be selected under the supervision of RONALD SMILEY INC., an independent judging organization whose decisions are final, by random drawings from valid entries postmarked by September 30, 1985, and received no later than October 7, 1985. Entry in this sweepstakes indicates your awareness of the Official Rules. Winners who are residents of Canada must answer correctly a time-related arithmetical skill-testing question to qualify. First Prize winner will be notified by certified mail and must submit an Affidavit of Compliance within 10 days of notification. Returned Affidavits or prizes that are refused or undeliverable will result in alternative names being randomly drawn. Winners may be asked for use of their name and photo at no additional compensation.

5. For a First Prize winner list, send a stamped self-addressed envelope postmarked by September 30, 1985. In Canada, mail to Silhouette Diamond Contest Winner, Suite 309, 238 Davenport Road, Toronto, Ontario M5R 1J6. In the United States, mail to Silhouette Diamond Contest Winner, P.O. Box 182, Bowling Green Station, New York, NY 10274. This offer will appear in Silhouette publications and at participating retailers. Offer void in Quebec and subject to all Federal, Provincial, State and Municipal laws and regulations and wherever prohibited or restricted by law.

SDR-A-1